KU-226-203

ABOUT THE AUTHOR

Claire Hennessy lives in Dublin and is currently studying (i.e. reading lots and lots and lots and lots) at Trinity College. She has never been given roses as a birthday gift, but can live with it. *That Girl* is her seventh book.

She can be found online at **www.clairehennessy.com**

This one's for Aisling, who is utterly fantabulous anyway, but was especially so re: this book. Happy margin-scribbling.
P.S. Mikey's babies. Dude.

1

Worrywart

I am not normally a neurotic person. Worrying is time-consuming and pointless and no way to live your life. You can worry all you like and it's not going to change anything. It's not going to stop people from hurting you or bad things from happening or unexpected disasters from being thrown in your path. It's sort of like impatience in that way – you can tap your foot and look at your watch all you want when someone or something is late, but it doesn't speed up time for you. All it does is stress you out.

Taking action is a much better way to live your life. I've tried explaining this to my brother Dan, who's doing his Leaving Cert this year, several thousand times. He's the perfect example of someone who worries so much that it's entirely counter-productive. He spends so much time on the verge of a nervous breakdown over points and college courses and CAO forms and past papers and all the rest that he hasn't got any time left to actually study.

Last week I tried for the hundredth time since the start of the school year – we're still only in December now – to remind him that he's a good student and that he's always done well on school exams and that he got great results in his Junior Cert. He promptly launched into one of his favourite rants: Why The Leaving Certificate Exam Is Ten Million Times Harder Than The Junior Cert And Is In Fact The Hardest Thing In The Universe Ever. And, all right, he's right about the Junior Cert not really mattering – a fact that our teachers were oh-so-thrilled to share with us less than a week after we got our results in September, bringing us down from the high we'd been on. They're slightly sadistic that way. But still, the Leaving can't be that hard. Thousands of students get through it every year without their heads exploding, after all. Our friend Michael is also in sixth year and is so far managing to remember that the apocalypse is not, in fact, nigh.

People completely lose it about exams. You can be the most confident person in the world and be reduced to mind-gone-blank jelly once you sit down and begin reading the test paper. I've seen it happen every year in school – people freeze up. Or they burst into tears. People you'd never think would ever get stressed out or even care about exams. People you think know everything and have no reason to worry. People who you can't help but feel sorry for even though all year they've annoyed you by asking stupid questions that have already been answered or by having pointless fights with the teachers or by showing off their extensive knowledge at every possible opportunity.

My friend Bonnie always panics in exams – and before them, too, the same way Dan does. We tried studying together for the Junior Cert last May, being really nerdy and getting a 'study group' going with a couple more girls from school, but it was the most pointless thing I've ever done. It was all about hoping certain questions wouldn't come up on the paper, when we could have spent the time just preparing for those questions instead. I mean, ok, I'm not that studious – I probably wouldn't have done that anyway. But if you're going to set aside two hours for studying something you might as well do it, instead of wasting that time. Or, if you're going to waste that time then you might as well waste it doing something fun, like going to the cinema or talking on the phone with a friend you haven't seen in ages and catching up on all their news.

Give me an exam to do and I probably won't get an A – unless it's languages, maybe – but I won't have a panic attack mid-page either.

Give me a party to organise, on the other hand, and welcome to Nervous Breakdown City.

Exams are easy to understand. You just need to speak the language. You need to know what's on the curriculum. What can be asked. What's usually asked. You need to understand how the paper is structured and how the marks are allocated, how to twist the questions to get the most out of your knowledge. There are rules and then there are exceptions to the rules and you need to know both. You need to jump through the right hoops instead of complaining about the hoops being there in the first place.

It's not quite like an equation, where one plus one equals two and the right mix of studying plus sleep plus exercise plus exam-taking skills gets you the grade you want. But it's close enough.

Parties, however, are *chaotic*. When you add all the elements in your exam equation together you'll get an answer close enough to round off to a whole number. When you add the elements of a party equation together, it can go anywhere. It can work out perfectly or it can blow up in your face. A location plus people plus food plus music equals – what? It can be anything. It can be the best night of your life or it can be a disaster. For starters, there are so many variables. The food might not be to everyone's taste. There might not be enough of it. There might be too much. The music might be spot-on or it could lead to war. The location could be a hip groovy apartment in the city centre, like where my cousin Sarah lives and has these fantastic dinner parties that Dan and I are sometimes invited to, or it could be – oh, say for example, an ordinary house in suburbia with parental supervision ensured at all times.

Because what more could a girl ask for on her sixteenth birthday? Parents watching over the proceedings, maybe even trying to make conversation with her friends – oh God. I mean, I'm not that embarrassed about them, really. Mum is not entirely out of touch with the world even if Jim doesn't have a clue about anything and still thinks I'm twelve years old (and since his idea of twelve involves treating people like they're four, we don't really communicate that well). I know that everyone thinks their parents are completely cringe-worthy, even when their friends find their quirks endearing or amusing or at the very least not as bad as what their own parents are like. I can handle Mum and Jim talking to Bonnie or Elaine or even Eddie (sure, it was awkward the first time they met, but the initial encounter between your boyfriend and your parents is always going to be painful, right? At least it wasn't as bad as the first time he met Dad) but that's different from them being around a group of my friends for the entire night. Five minutes of conversation upon arrival, or talking in the car, or chatting over dinner, is ok. It's fine. Constant checking in on us because they're terrified of everyone getting drunk is not fine.

Jim, my 'beloved' stepfather, is always finding articles in the newspaper about binge drinking and teenage alcoholism and all that stuff, and saving them to show Mum. He also thoughtfully tapes documentaries on the subject for her to watch. I am convinced that she'd be less uptight about alcohol if he didn't constantly remind her of the dangers and all the extreme cases that neither of them seem to think I'm smart enough to avoid.

They worry and worry and it's completely pointless. They're worried that I will spend my birthday party off my face. They are worried that the guests will drink and that their parents will call them up the next morning and it'll be a huge scandal and Mum and Jim will seem like the most irresponsible parents in the universe. They're worried that I'll become an alcoholic if I have a single drink, because apparently I'm that silly and stupid and have no concept of moderation.

I want to tell them that I'm already over that stupid binge-drinking phase. That I had my first drink with Dan and Michael at thirteen. That when I was fourteen, Bonnie and I used to go drinking in fields with these guys she went to primary school with, and we'd stay over at her house because her mum and dad went out on Saturday nights and got home late enough to give us enough time to go out, get pissed, come back to the house and fall asleep without them ever realising we'd left the house. We did various stupid drunk things like kissing people we weren't even remotely attracted to and calling up friends or acquaintances and slurring things down the phone that we'd later regret, plus the typical practical jokes that seem like a fantastic idea at the time and are decidedly less funny the following morning when you have your next-door neighbour's garden gnome sitting at the foot of your bed. For example.

I want to tell Mum and Jim that I've already done that drinking-just-to-get-drunk thing, where you down a bottle of spirits in a ridiculously short space of time and end up throwing it all up a couple of hours later, that I've already moved on from that phase and drink sensibly now. But they would collapse in horror at the very idea of it, and probably never let me see Bonnie again, and they'd still freak out over the idea of an almost-sixteen-year-old drinking at all, because if the law says you have to be over eighteen then clearly the law must be right and no one is allowed think otherwise.

You'd think they'd credit me with enough intelligence not to bring the sort of people who think it'd be ok to get completely twisted with someone else's parents around home with me, but apparently nothing less than total supervision will convince them that my friends are not a bunch of alcoholic drug fiends. Oh, and sex maniacs, too. Upstairs will be off-limits for the boys, so that there can be no illicit bedroom-based activities under their roof. There is part of me that wishes I had a whole bunch of lesbian friends who could have an orgy upstairs, just to make a point about Mum and Jim's antiquated ultra-conservative view of the world. Tragically, I do not, and I am fairly sure a week is not long enough to acquire said friends.

I can't change this. I can't do anything about it. It's not like worrying about exams, where you're taking time away from studying by getting all neurotic about it. I can't persuade Mum and Jim to turn into more normal parental figures for a night. I've tried. I've tried talking them into being less overprotective and actually considering treating me like an almost grown-up, but to no avail. I'm fifteen-going-on-sixteen and they look at me and see a child.

I can't just decide not to have a party. The invitations have already been sent out. Elaine designed them, being both helpful and ten times more artistic than I can ever hope to be, and I posted them last Friday. Jim dropped the bombshell on me after that, saying it so casually, like of *course* he and Mum were going to be around the whole time instead of making themselves scarce. He sounded surprised that I hadn't assumed this, shocked and appalled that I had actually considered the possibility of being treated like a teenager instead of a toddler. Would it kill them to go out for a couple of hours, or even just watch some TV up in their bedroom?

I don't think I'm being unreasonable about that. Unreasonable would involve bursting into tears and slamming doors and screaming at Jim, which, ok, was pretty much exactly what happened when he came into my room this morning and told me to turn down my music and reminded me that there was no way I could have it that loud for the party, because the neighbours would complain.

Unreasonable would involve not wanting to talk to my friend Orla, who's chosen going to a concert over celebrating my birthday, ever again. Or crying over the computer freezing up just when I've finished making up my playlist. Or wanting to scream at Eddie simply because he doesn't realise what this is doing to me, even though I haven't explained it to him and cannot logically expect him to be psychic.

I know unreasonable, and irrational, and crazy. Every time I think about my birthday party, I live them.

2

Telltale

One of the reasons I wish I wasn't having my birthday party this week is because we're not in school. Now, naturally enough, normally not being in school is a good thing, even though it's not really like we have the week off. It's one of the weeks we have allocated for work experience, and I'm spending it in a school – if not our school – anyway, but everyone's been looking forward to our week not-in-school for ages now.

This means, however, that I'm not going to be seeing people every day, and not checking in on who's coming on Saturday night or not, and not talking about it with people. Not getting reassurances from Bonnie and Deirdre and the others. There are people like Carrie whose mobile numbers I don't have yet but who I've been getting along really well with this year now that we're all mixed up for our as-part-of-the-unique-opportunities-afforded-by-Transition-Year activities, people I'd like to text and remind but can't. I'm cut off from the everyday and I find myself with no idea of what's appropriate or not. I know I could talk to Deirdre about what outfit to wear or to Dawn about what sort of music to play if we were sitting around at break time having our usual twenty-to-eleven chat, but it's harder to communicate with text messages, harder to really talk about things.

Some people conduct entire relationships through text messages, deal with all the issues through the phone, and never talk about it in person. Eddie's old girlfriend Laura broke up with him via a text message. A single text, not even a series of them – she told him she'd cheated on him and that it was best if they ended things right now, all in 160 characters. He hates her more for that than he does for actually cheating on him. Eddie likes his big romantic gestures – like, he took me out to a restaurant to celebrate our six-month anniversary (even though technically anniversaries are counted in years and someone needs to invent a new word for things that are counted in months – monthiversary, maybe?), the sort with candles and flowers in vases and all that stuff. Text messages do not fit into his concept of romance. I like that about him.

And I get it, too. That's why I can't discuss anything party-related through text messages. I freeze up because I can't see faces, expressions, body language, and I need those things to communicate about important things.

I can't believe I'm the sort of girl who thinks a party is the most important thing in the world. I mean, I'm not. Not normally. Maybe I'm just possessed. Possessed by the ghost of someone who never lived to make it to her own sixteenth birthday, maybe?

That's creepy and morbid. I'm not going to think about it. And I'm not going to think about the party. I am going to think about – the Great Famine.

This is what the fifth class that I am helping out with this week – really, I'm just standing around and feeling useless a lot of the time – are learning about this morning.

They have questions to answer and it's all based on the stuff in their book, but they still put their hands up to ask things anyway. Miss McCabe is correcting homework so I'm on answer duty.

I haven't opened a history book since I started secondary school, picking an extra language and music over history for my Junior Cert subjects. Every bit of knowledge I have is from when I was their age.

Fortunately, most of their questions can be answered by telling them to read carefully over the last few pages again, which from their reactions you'd think was the hardest thing in the world to do. They're reminding me a bit of Dan, actually, especially this one girl who keeps sighing and glaring at me for not giving her the answer straight off.

She puts her hand up and I go over again, crouching down to her height. I can't believe I was once that small, that I fitted into these faux-wood plastic chairs. No wonder girls get so neurotic about their weight. We expand like crazy once the teenage years hit.

"You know the coffin ships?" she says.

"Mmm-hmm?" I do know. I think. Big ships. Crammed with people emigrating. Many died before reaching the destination due to bad conditions. Please don't ask me anything more specific than that. I wish Elaine was here. She's the history expert, in comparison to me, anyway.

"How many people went on them?"

"Um. Is that one of the questions?"

"No. I'm just curious." She shrugs.

I am highly doubtful of her interest in history. This is only day two and already I know she's not exactly passionate about her schoolwork. She spent yesterday morning staring out of the window and looking bored and world-weary.

"Is it not in the book?" I try.

"Nope." She stares at me, challenging me.

"Right. Do you mean overall or per ship?"

"Both."

I hate her. "Per ship, I guess they crammed in as many people as they could. It probably depended on the size of the ship. Overall, I have no idea. Ask your teacher."

"Why don't you know?"

"Because I don't take history."

"Yeah, but you must have done this when you were in school. How old are you?"

Is this a question I have to answer? Is this appropriate? I have no idea.

"Sixteen," I say. Not quite, not yet, but I want to assert whatever minimal authority I have here.

She looks at me scornfully. "I would have thought you were, like, thirteen."

I have no idea what to say to that. I blink at her, stand up, and go over to answer someone else's question. This kid is one of the nice ones – sweet, quiet, appropriately in awe of someone old enough to be in here on work experience but young enough to be cool. I idolised teenagers when I was this age. I thought they were the coolest things ever, imagining that it was so close to being grown-up that you could hardly tell the difference, that it would really be the best time of your life.

Was I that obnoxious when I was – what, ten, eleven? And once I ask myself that question I'm not sure I want to think about it for too long.

I remember being in fifth class. I was a good kid. Well-behaved, average, and – not what my teacher had expected. At all.

She'd been warned about me. It's funny to think about it now – strange funny – while sitting in a room filled with fifth class pupils.

The year before, my parents split up. I don't remember fourth class very well. For a while I Acted Out, apparently. Mum tells these stories about me at that age, now that people can laugh about it because I got over it, but it's like she's telling them about someone else. My friends from primary school can tell them too. And I know how stories change and morph and twist with every retelling. I have no idea where the kernel of truth in each of them is.

I don't want to think about that. I can't change it. There's no point in analysing it and reliving it and worrying about it now. It happened. It's over. I was ten years old and now I'm going to be sixteen and childhood is *over*.

I wonder if the brat-girl has problems at home. Real problems, maybe, like abusive parents or a death in the family or something, not just the typical run-of-the-mill separation-segueing-into-divorce. I wonder if

I am being too sensitive. I wonder if people need a reason to be like that or if sometimes it's just the way they are.

At break time Miss McCabe asks me how I'm getting on. She mentions brat-girl, also known as Pearl, and I ask if she's normally much trouble.

"She was sort of rude," I say, and it feels like telling on her, almost. "She probably doesn't even realise that she's behaving that way," I add in an attempt to get her off the hook.

Miss McCabe nods.

I know what she's thinking. The kids don't have to respect me. Why should they? I'm not a qualified teacher, I'm not doing anything important. I'm just here because I have to be somewhere for the week, and because this school has an arrangement with several TY programmes in the area, and because I like kids and this place seemed like the best place to be.

That's the problem with work experience, though. You're not qualified to do anything crucial, so you end up doing bits and pieces but nothing that really matters, so you don't actually get a taste of what the job is like. The only way you really get to find out what a job is like is by doing it – and you can't do that until you have the qualification, a qualification that you might decide wasn't even worth the trouble.

After their break they take out their maths books.

Pearl's hand goes up within what feels like seconds.

"I'm finished," she announces.

I look over her sums even though it's Miss McCabe who has the power of ticking with her red pen and writing 'v.g.' on the page.

"What's seven times eight?" she asks me while I'm checking her long division.

"Fifty-four."

"Oh my God. *No.* It's fifty-six. *Babies* know that. My little *sister* knows that."

"I was distracted doing this," I say calmly, pointing to her copybook. At least, I mean to say it calmly, but I'm not particularly tranquil today.

"Sure," she says and rolls her eyes.

I want to slap her. I actually want to slap her. She looks so smug and so superior and she's younger than me, she's a little kid, and she thinks she's better than me because I slipped up on my times-tables. I can do quadratic equations and co-ordinate geometry and she thinks she's brilliant because she knows how to multiply single digits.

"You are not a very nice person," I say instead. I think about how I could have said something much more offensive and apt, but as she goes up to get Miss McCabe to correct her work I realise that it's still not on, telling a kid that, especially when you're just a student yourself.

I worry that she will tell Miss McCabe what I said and I'll get in trouble for it.

I hate being here. I thought I'd like this. I like kids. When I was little I always begged Mum and Dad to have another kid so that I'd have someone to take care of (though of course, having another child wasn't exactly at the top of their To Do list). I love baby-sitting – I always play games with the kids and listen to their stories and take them outside and actually pay attention to them instead of just sticking in a video the way some people do. I love being around them and seeing the world through their eyes.

I thought I'd be good at this, but I don't seem to be doing a very good job at all. I bet Pearl would agree.

3

Mouse

I am very grateful when it's lunchtime. It's only half an hour, but it means there's only two hours left when we come back. And then I can go home and get away from being useless. I can't wait.

There are other girls from my school doing work experience here too, but they're the ones that I don't really talk to. They're the ones who are always getting in trouble and who are only staying in school because their parents are making them, who would much rather get a job and move in with their boyfriends or whatever it is they have planned for themselves. They talk back to the teachers and never have their homework done. Some of them get stressed out over exams but mostly they stick with not caring, in that sort of loud elaborate making-sure-everyone-knows-they-don't-care way.

They're not the type of girls I'd have imagined would turn up here. In a school. With small children. I can't see them actually wanting to be primary school teachers or even vaguely considering it as a career option. I can't see them being patient and gentle with kids.

But then again what do I know? Maybe they're brilliant. Maybe they would deal with someone like Pearl much more effectively than I can ever hope to, or maybe they wouldn't even have to deal with her because she'd respect them. Maybe I'm just so obviously not the super-cool teenage type that even ten- and eleven-year-olds can pick up on it.

They're all sitting outside together, eating lunch and smoking and talking. I walk past them, eyes straight ahead, and head towards the shopping centre five minutes down the road. We're allowed into the staff room during breaks. I thought they'd be in there, which is why I'm not. It's December, cold out, but the sun is shining today, at least. I still wish I had my gloves with me. And that they were all inside and not looking at me walking off to lunch all by myself.

I know I shouldn't care what they think. Or maybe I should believe that they have better things to do with their time than think about me – even though they don't, because all anyone in school ever does is talk about other people and their shortcomings. I just don't like the idea that they're going to see me as some poor friendless creature who has no life whatsoever, all because my friends are doing work experience somewhere else. They're not going to ponder the matter carefully and realise that I do have friends but that unlike them I put what I wanted to do this week ahead of wanting to hang out with people I know. They're just going to think I'm a sad loner. And who knows, maybe this party will prove them right.

I get in line at the deli. I'm in the mood for potato wedges – something to warm me up, something comforting.

"He-ey!" It's Dawn. Her greetings always have more syllables than other people's do. "What are you doing here?"

"Getting wedges," I say, nodding towards the counter.

"Oooh, good choice! Are you – where are you doing your work experience, again?"

"St Joseph's."

"Oh, right, of course! How's it going? What are the kids like?"

"They're ok. How's the office thing going?" Dawn is spending the week at a solicitor's office, just down the road. She has no intention of going into law, but a friend of her dad works there and is going to pay her for the week, even though that's not supposed to happen with work experience, so she leapt at that opportunity.

"Oh my God, it's so boring! You wouldn't believe it. And, oh my God, I broke the photocopier this morning. It was so embarrassing, seriously. They all think I'm, like, retarded."

I flinch when she says that. It is not an inherently offensive word, retarded. From the Latin *tardus* – slow. She means they think she is slow. She is not trying to piss off people who might actually care about using terms like that because they actually have to deal with people who have learning disabilities.

I think about one of the kids I baby-sit, Kira, who has Down's Syndrome. If any of the other kids I know used that word, I'd tell them not to. If any of the kids in the class said it I – I don't know. I don't know if I have that authority over them. I do know I certainly don't have authority over Dawn.

She keeps talking. "But there's this really cute guy there who I was talking to today, so that's something, at least . . . I mean, obviously I'm not going to *do* anything about it, but you know, it's fun."

I don't know. Dawn has a boyfriend she's crazy about but she still talks about cute guys as though she's single, sort of wistfully at times.

"How's Jason?" I ask. That's the boyfriend. The one she is supposedly madly in love with.

"Oh, he's fine. The usual, you know? Oh, oh my God, he got us tickets to the Philosophers thing on Saturday, isn't that great?"

The Philosophers. A band, not actual professional philosophers. It's the Existentialism tour, to promote their new album. It's the concert Orla's going to. The concert that's happening the same night as my birthday party.

"Yeah," I say, waiting for the follow-up apology, waiting for the 'Oh my God, that's the same night as your party! I can't believe I forgot!', waiting for something.

Nothing.

I pay for the potato wedges and wait for Dawn to get her order. There are benches down near the bookshop that we can sit on while we eat.

Except it turns out Jason's waiting for her. She smiles, says a cheery goodbye to me and then slides her hand into his. They walk away and she rests her head on his shoulder, like she's incapable of supporting herself.

I sit down on my own and start eating. I feel horribly alone. Everyone seems to have someone. The loud girls have each other. Dawn has Jason. The little girl walking by has her mother's hand to hold onto.

That old man has his son walking alongside him.

Everyone always goes on about how alone they feel whenever they're single. But you can have a boyfriend and still be alone sometimes, unless you're glued at the hip like Jason and Dawn. It wouldn't even occur to me to ask Eddie to come and meet me for lunch – I mean, it wouldn't be worth his time, it'd take so long to travel to and from his school that there'd be no point.

I wonder if that means that Jason and Dawn have a better relationship than me and Eddie. But then again, Dawn still flirts with guys and comments on how attractive they are, and I haven't been attracted to anyone else ever since Eddie and I got together.

It was last New Year's Eve that it all happened. Mum and Dad always used to go to this party that friends of theirs from college have every year, but I guess they decided Dad got these friends and the party invitations when they got divorced, because Mum and Jim now spend New Year's at home together watching TV. Dad goes every year with his 'lady friend' Annelise and invites me and Dan along. Last year Dan refused – he goes through stages of not talking to Dad – but I went along because I didn't have anything else to do and because the year before I had realised that one of the boys who was always there had suddenly developed a personality and good looks, and I had vague intentions of chatting him up.

Instead, I got talking to Eddie, who I'd never seen before – his family had moved in next door to the hosts over the summer – and was quickly charmed. We talked about music and computer games, two topics I'm used to talking about with guys (Dan and Michael consider themselves experts on both). I might look like a clueless teenybopper type sometimes (this is what happens when you wear blonde hair in pigtails, it's simply unavoidable) but I do know what I'm talking about when it comes to those two areas. Dawn – along with a lot of other girls I know – likes having boys explain things to her and playing the ditz, but I'd rather be on equal footing if at all possible. There's no point in pretending you don't know about something when there are so many things in the world that you genuinely won't be knowledgeable about.

Fencing, for example – one of Eddie's interests. I was entirely ignorant. I didn't even know people still fenced these days. He told me he was into it; I made a joke about duelling for my honour and he looked embarrassed but said that he would, actually. It was sweet. I liked that he wasn't overly confident and didn't try to maul me even though across the room the boy that I'd meant to chat up was doing just that to another girl, not to mention the way the adults were behaving. At midnight I kissed him and we started off the year together. (And twenty minutes later Dad ventured over to be introduced to "this young gentleman", having witnessed exactly how we had begun the year. Which is not really the sort of thing you want to happen at that stage in a relationship, but we survived it.)

I was so confident then, so sure that I could kiss him without worrying about it, so secure in myself that I didn't need to censor myself to make myself seem like the sort of girl he might be interested in. I knew that he liked me and – best of all – I knew that I was being myself, regardless of what he thought. I truly believed in the idea that if he didn't like me for me, he wasn't worth having around.

So how did I get to be this mousy creature who can't even stand up to her friend and confront her about using inappropriate words or not bothering to remember important things like where people are doing their work experience or what day their birthday party's on?

Exactly when did I become the sort of girl who can't bear being alone for a single thirty-minute lunch break? The sort of meek timid creature who cares what everyone – not just the people she likes, but *everyone* – thinks of her? The kind of girl who gets upset over what a random ten-year-old with an obvious chip on her shoulder says to her? How the hell did I get here?

I want to run after Dawn and Jason and yell at her for not remembering that my birthday party is this weekend. I want to scream at her for never remembering anything about anyone else except the boys she's interested in. I want to tear her hair out, a clump for every time she's said something that irritated me but that I let go for the sake of not causing a fuss. All of these minor annoyances flood my brain and I'm angry and hurt over the most trivial things, like that time last year when she needed to ask who'd been at the cinema one weekend a few weeks previously because she couldn't remember. Then I just dismissed it as Dawn being Dawn – forgetful and scatterbrained and just not the sort of person who remembers details the way I do. Now it makes me feel insignificant. Not important enough to be remembered.

Not important enough to miss a concert for. Not important enough to make an effort for, on the one day that's all mine, the only day of the year where it's all about me.

I think that's it, the birthday thing. Why it drives me so crazy. Other days – Valentine's Day, Christmas – are celebrated by everyone or almost everyone. You can't help but be aware of them. The shops tell you, so you don't have to remember. But there are no "Kim's Birthday!" banners up, no special gift sets for the occasion of my sixteenth birthday. This one is the sort of thing I have to do the promotional work for all by myself. I have to be the special attraction to draw people in.

And being the special attraction is one thing when it's you and a couple of kids and you're making up a story and they're going to love you anyway because you're a big girl and you listen to them and they like you, or when it's you and your boyfriend and he's chosen to be with you because he's mad about you, but when you have to be the special attraction for lots of people, all with their different interests and personalities and lives – that's when it starts getting complicated.

And instead of rising to meet the occasion, I seem to be shrinking, growing smaller and smaller so that soon there'll be nothing left of me.

4

Little Sister

On Wednesday afternoon the kids are painting. It's times like this when I miss primary school. I'm useless with a paintbrush but it doesn't matter when you're little, it doesn't mean that you can't still do it in school and absolutely love it.

When you're little the world is full of possibilities and you think you can do anything. At some point that changes and you have to pick just one or two things that you want to do, that you can do really well. Like Dan trying to decide what college course he really wants, what one thing he's going to choose above all the others, and even then his choices are limited because of the subjects he picked to do for his Leaving. Kids seem to be able to do anything and everything.

I feel sort of old, but then young at the same time – young because I'm squeezing out paint onto palettes for the kids and they're giggling at the sound and I have to stop myself from smiling too. Young because when Pearl runs into me 'accidentally' and gets paint on my clothes, I can't give out to her. That's Miss McCabe's job. There's a proper grown-up in the room and I have to just accept her apology and ignore the smirk on her face.

If I was babysitting I'd make her apologise properly, or send her to her room, or take away her paints. Here I have someone else looking over my shoulder and I have no power whatsoever.

And paint all over me.

When I get home, the doorbell rings before I have a chance to change. Mum and Jim are still at work and Dan has left a note saying that he's studying at Saoirse's house this afternoon. His school finishes early on Wednesdays – they're supposed to stay for sports but Dan hasn't done that since he was twelve. I was so disappointed when I found out my school didn't have a similar arrangement, despite all their blathering about a well-rounded education. We are encouraged to do sports, as long as it doesn't interfere with our all-important learning-from-books experiences.

It's Michael. "Hey, Kimmie," he says.

Very few people can get away with calling me Kimmie. Jim tried it once and I screamed at him, because it was like he was trying to be my dad, fill this place in my life that didn't need filling. It's for family only – I know Jim counts as family now, but I still don't want him using pet names for me – and I guess Michael gets away with it because he's been Dan's best friend for ages and he's known me for almost as long.

There's this picture of us from the summer when I was seven and they were nine up in the kitchen, the three fair heads together making us look like one big happy family instead of two kids from a marriage about to shatter and one kid from an entirely different family. People always used to think we were all related. Cousins, at the very least.

"Is Dan around?" he asks as I put on the kettle. When Michael comes over and Mum and Jim are around, they ask him if he wants coffee. I just make it. I know the answer is always yes.

"Nah, he's over at Saoirse's. There's a note around somewhere. Who's Saoirse, anyway?"

Michael's found the note. "Studying?" He laughs. "Yeah, right. Saoirse's this girl he met a couple of weeks ago when we went out –"

"Girlfriend? Almost-girlfriend?"

"Almost, I think. They're definitely not studying over there, anyway."

"He never tells me anything," I sigh. Ok, that's not fair. Dan and I do talk. It's just sometimes he refuses to talk to me about girls. I rely on Michael to keep me updated, which he thoughtfully always does. Whoever said that gossip is an entirely female activity was sorely mistaken.

"Never tells me anything either. I thought he was going to be around this evening," he says.

"You know what he's like, though. Saoirse probably has him whipped."

I make him coffee and make hot chocolate for myself.

"You can head home if you like," I say, "if you just wanted to talk to Dan. I won't take it personally, promise."

He takes a sip. "Trying to get rid of me?" He grins, and I smile back. "Love the arty look, by the way."

"It's very me, isn't it?"

"Kids?"

"Yeah."

"I miss primary school art," he says.

"Me too."

We sit in silence for a moment before he asks, "How are things with Eddie?"

I shrug. "The usual. How's your love life going, mister? What are you doing when my brother's picking up girls, huh?"

He sighs. "How about if we don't talk about that."

I nod. "Ok." And then, "It's not the end of the world to be single, you know."

"Depends on what you want."

Yeah. Good point. I don't push it. Michael hasn't had a girlfriend since things ended between him and Caitriona last summer. I think it gets to him sometimes, especially when there are girls in the picture for Dan.

"How's the party-planning going?" he wants to know, and we end up taking our mugs upstairs to my room so he can offer advice on the music situation.

Dan is snobbish about his music. Michael is even worse. They mocked me mercilessly for liking pop music when I was younger, and for a while I just completely copied them in their taste, agreeing with everything they said instead of having opinions of my own. Now I'm over the hero-worship thing. Now I am at the point in my life where I can disagree with them.

"I'm not putting 'Giving Up' on this, Mikey."

"Why not? It's one of the greatest songs ever recorded!"

"It's depressing!"

"It's brilliant!"

We're sitting on my bed, me with my laptop – Dan's old one, slightly the worse for wear but still functioning, mostly – balanced on my knees and

Michael looking over my shoulder as I scroll through the list of songs.

I can feel his breath on my neck and it suddenly makes me shiver a little.

"Cold?"

"A little," I say, passing the computer over to him and getting up to get another jumper. I take the paint-splattered one off first, pulling it over my head and leaving my hair in a mess, and pull on this oversized black thing I've had for ages. It's one of the most comfortable things I own, the sort of thing I only ever wear around the house because it's so shapeless.

Michael has seen me in my dressing-gown first thing in the morning. I am not particularly worried about how sloppy I look right now.

I mean, it's not as though he's somebody I need to impress. Or want to.

Even if Elaine's theory is right, which it isn't, it doesn't mean anything in terms of my interaction with him.

I have a boyfriend. I have Eddie.

Not all friendships with boys have to be laden with something more. It's always annoyed me when people assume that a friendship with a boy means that you're attracted to one another. As though anything more than being on nodding terms with a member of the opposite sex means that it absolutely has to be heading towards romance. It's ridiculous.

I mean, of course I liked him a little bit when I was younger. It's practically required that little girls have a bit of a crush on their older brother's friends, especially when the only boys you ever get to see in school are the middle-aged caretakers. It doesn't mean that I'm interested in him now. I'm not a kid anymore.

I sit down on the bed again. "What have you done?" I sigh as I take back the computer. He's been adding all of his favourites – not necessarily the same thing as my favourites – to the birthday playlist.

"Kimmie. Trust me."

"Nope," I say, and delete half of what he's added. The rest can stay – the ones that aren't all about gloom and doom.

We keep going, bickering over the quality of the songs and the appropriateness of them for a birthday party. I start yawning after a while – despite the short days, the work experience thing is still tiring me out a little. It doesn't help that I haven't been sleeping the best this week.

"You need coffee," Michael decides. Coffee is Michael's cure for everything, from hangovers to broken hearts. The first time he convinced me to try it was right after Tom and I broke up. I remain unconvinced of its magical properties, though shuddering at that first taste did at least distract me from the hopeless weeping.

We're sitting in the kitchen, Michael with his black coffee and me with my coffee plus chocolate flavouring (my compromise between 'real' coffee and chocolate drinks), when Jim and Mum get home.

My mother and James Murphy – proof that office romances can last. Also proof that going out with someone from work means that you turn into someone who talks about nothing else but work and work colleagues and office gossip, even at home. (When they're not being paranoid about my alcoholic friends and all that, of course.) I think that would drive me crazy, but it seems to work for them. They're happy together.

"Hi, Michael. How are you doing? How's the studying going?"

Michael regales them with tales of school while Jim makes a pot of tea. We consume far too much caffeine in this house, I think, and turn down the offer of a cup in the hope it will improve my chances of sleeping tonight.

I watch him talk, gesture, be as at ease with them as I am, as Dan is. Michael, my sort-of big brother. It doesn't have to be anything more than that. It's fine just as it is.

5

Insomniac

What keeps me awake on Wednesday night is the whole concept of *mixing.*

Parties bring together people who might otherwise never meet, people who have nothing in common except knowing the host. A single mutual friend. That's it.

Parties are when the people you usually keep apart are brought together in the same room, where the boundaries that exist are broken down. They're your entire life on display, a round-up of all the people who are important to you. They're your history, laid out for everyone to see and investigate.

There are people coming to this thing who I knew from primary school, friends like Mandy who know what I was like right after my parents split up and who can tell stories about the time when I was six and threw up on the teacher's shoes, or the time I fainted on stage when our third class put on a play and the whole thing had to stop while I was carried off and how I was subsequently referred to as 'Sleeping Beauty' for the rest of the year, which as a nickname wouldn't have been too traumatic were it not for several of the boys being typical boys of that age and changing it to 'Sleeping Ugly'.

There's Bonnie, who lived through most of the Silly Things Kim Has Done When Drunk stories, and I can't decide whether these stories are better or worse than the stories about me as a bratty ten-year-old, in large part because the same kind of memory gaps and blurriness occur when thinking about such events. There's Deirdre, who was around for the summer I went out with Tom and did some very foolish things. (I was a fourteen-year-old in love, or what I thought was love at the time. Foolishness was bound to ensue, and oh how it did, in the form of that dreadful song I wrote for him, to name one example. Having at this stage been highly influenced by Dan and Michael's taste, you'd think I'd have written something a little better than 'And I'm just so blue / when not with you'. Or that line about birds and the sky and sunsets.) And then there are people like Carrie and Elaine who have a certain idea of what I'm like, an idea that will probably be completely turned on its head by the end of the party.

Mum and Dan have known me all of my life. Michael and Susan from down the road have known me for almost that long.

All of these people with their stories to tell and their ideas of what I'm like, all mixing together.

I know. I know. They will have other things to talk about apart from me. I am not the centre of the universe. I'm not even close. I know this. I'm not even as important as a concert. But I still can't stop thinking about it, worrying about it.

And then – what if they don't talk to each other at all? What if they don't get along? I mean, if I thought that everyone was perfectly suited to everyone else and that it's the perfect mix, I would have introduced everyone a lot sooner.

I think about last year, my fifteenth birthday. Some of the schools around here had Christmas exams on top of mocks, so I went out for pizza with the girls from my school to celebrate the actual day, and met up with the primary school crowd a week later for a joint birthday/Christmas celebration. That was before Eddie, before Elaine. That was a non-stressful birthday. No mixing, no worries.

What if, what if, what if. What if Eddie hears stories

about me, gets to learn things about me that I haven't shared with him? What if he pities me for ever having been so drunk that I had to be carried home, or what if he's disgusted by it? He prides himself on holding his alcohol, on not doing stupid things when inebriated. Bonnie could tell him about, say, the time I kissed that guy who looked a whole lot older than thirteen but really wasn't. I had just turned fourteen then, so it wasn't the biggest deal in the world, but at the time it seemed like it was, especially when I thought I was being so grown-up by kissing someone who looked at least fifteen. It is not a story I am particularly fond of hearing. And Eddie's the kind of guy who's able to tell these stories about other people, not be the one with a starring role in them.

What if Elaine thinks that all the rest of my friends are boring or superficial or have something else wrong with them? I don't know what Elaine's friends from school are like, what crowd she hangs out with on a nine-to-four basis. I've only ever met them briefly, not enough times to get to know them properly. What if she realises that my friends from school are exactly the type of people that her school crowd would mock mercilessly? What's that going to say about me?

What if the friends who haven't met Eddie yet don't like him? What if they think he's too tall or not cool enough or not good-looking or just somehow not my type? What if they start talking about my bad taste in guys behind my back and secretly judge me for it?

What if Bonnie and Elaine don't get along? Or what if they get along really well and decide that they should be friends and I'm not interesting enough for them? What if they start making plans that don't include me and I don't realise and it's only when I run into the two of them shopping or something that it hits me that I'm just not cool enough for them any more? Or maybe they would include me at the start, because they're nice, but it would only be out of sympathy and pity, which would be the worst thing in the world.

What if Eddie's friends think it's a childish party because there's no alcohol, there's parental supervision and no chance of going upstairs for bedroom-related fun? I know what their parties are like. They're loud and they're crazy and they'll get bored at this kind of party, the kind where you can't knock back half a bottle of something vile in one go or tear the house apart.

What if everyone keeps saying no like Orla and Dawn because they have concerts to go to or exams to study for or Christmas stuff to do? What if no one shows up? What if it's just me and Eddie and the family and that's it? What if people just don't want to bother making the effort?

I try to remember all the parties that have been

planned, ever. I know there are ones that I've missed, for real reasons like being on a trip or having already had plans, and not-so-real reasons like not really being in the party mood and wanting to stay at home on a particular night.

Why didn't I ever realise how important it is to go to these things? Why can't I remember the ones that I ignored, now that it feels like I'm always going to remember Orla and Dawn not showing up? Is the real reason they're not coming to do with the fact that at some stage I failed to turn up to something they'd planned?

Suddenly I see the world as nothing more than a series of unspoken agreements. There's a seedy underbelly to all those cheerful text messages that proclaim "hope 2 c u dere!" What it really means, "I'll scratch your back if you'll scratch mine". It means, "If you don't come to my party I'll boycott yours".

No one told me these rules, no one ever explained this system to me. Everyone already knows these things and it's just me who never realised, and now it's too late.

What if we run out of food? What if there's too much food and everyone thinks how pathetic it is that we ordered more food than necessary because clearly there are not enough guests to eat this much food after lots of people decided not to bother coming?

What if Mandy has one of her dramatic break-ups? Every time I see Mandy she has a new boyfriend and she usually breaks up with them via a far-too-public fight. Mandy has no qualms about making a scene. She doesn't even see it that way – it's more that she does what she has to do and it doesn't matter where or when it happens.

I don't want her to do that this time, even though normally it doesn't get to me the way it does to other people. I don't think it's inherently wrong to have a public break-up – maybe a little tactless, but not the end of the world, and much better than waiting for the right moment to end things and find yourself still together further down the road because the right moment refuses to present itself – but I don't want the sort of scene that Mum and Jim will remind me about for years to come.

What do I want? I want everyone to behave and I want everyone to have fun and I want interesting things to happen without everything getting out of control and I'm not sure these things can coexist.

I want the world to go on as it was and for nothing to change, for everything to be ok.

Why does it feel as though this party is going to turn things upside down? Other people don't worry about parties this much. They can't. Do they? Does it prevent them from sleeping and keep them tossing and turning as though something catastrophic is about to happen?

Why have I turned into a worrier, a crazy insomniac obsessed with something as relatively trivial as a party? It's just a party. It's not the end of the world. These things are supposed to be fun, not a death sentence. Worrying is pointless. Why don't I trust the things I normally believe in? Why don't they seem to apply in this situation?

I reach out for my phone and send Eddie a text message. It's late but he's a night person; he might still be up, playing computer games or chatting online.

I'll talk to him, let him reassure me. Let myself be comforted and soothed. Isn't that what boyfriends are for? Why do we get into relationships if we can't turn to the other person when we need them? Wouldn't I normally tell someone who can't tell her boyfriend anything that she shouldn't be in a relationship if they're not communicating? What happened to that girl?

The sound is turned off but I see the screen lighting up. He's calling.

"Hi," I say.

"Hey. Is everything ok?" He's concerned. He cares. He doesn't mind that it's late and that most of the people in this time zone are sound asleep.

I'm lucky. I know that. I do.

"Everything's fine," I say. "I just can't sleep, and I wanted to talk to you . . . if you were up. I didn't wake you up, did I?"

"No, it's fine. Want me to sing you a lullaby?"

I giggle, and I can hear him laugh too. "That's ok," I say, "just – talk to me."

So he does, relating some story about school and a crazy teacher, and it distracts me from these night-time worries, and when the call ends I realise that I didn't mention, not even once, just how much this party thing is bothering me.

So much for communication.

6

Troublemaker

I walk into the classroom on Thursday morning powered entirely by coffee. Michael would be so proud. I didn't even put the chocolate flavouring in. Not even milk. Just pure coffee.

The last time I had a sleepless night and then had to face the day ahead instead of sleeping through the morning was last summer. Not sleeping because you've been sneaking out is so much better than not sleeping because you've been worrying.

I miss last summer. The Gaeltacht part of it, I mean. I hated the college – it was incredibly strict and the activities were just irritating, as though they'd been designed for kids instead of teenagers – but the people were great. Not all of them – there were some real bitches there, including my roommates – but on the second day I got talking to Elaine and a few others, and we stuck together for the rest of the course. We all still keep in touch, some more than others, but Elaine's the only one who lives near me, so she's turned into a real friend, the sort you can invite over or ask to help out with birthday party invitations.

The last time I was this tired was right after that night we had this party outdoors, in the woods near where we were staying. There was dancing to real music, the kind we weren't allowed listen to in the houses or in the college because it wasn't in Irish, and passing around a couple of bottles that people had packed for such an eventuality. We told ghost stories and played Truth or Dare and all those silly games that are the most fun things in the world when it's late at night and you're slightly tipsy and you really like the people you're surrounded by.

Sometimes I think the more you get to know people, the less you appreciate them and see their good points. Friends become people that stay in your life because you're used to them instead of it being about genuinely wanting to be in each other's company.

I feel like there's a lot more I could do with that train of thought, but at the moment all I want to do is sleep.

It's a pity fifth class are too old for nap-time. I think it would be very beneficial. My pillow seems like the most appealing thing in the universe right now.

For a moment I think today might be a Pearl-free day, but it turns out she's just late. Typical. She'll grow up to be one of those troublemakers who surprise people like me by doing work experience in a school, I bet. She has that look about her, that hard look in her eyes that says she's not going to listen to anyone who tries to tell her what to do, and if she absolutely has to, she'll sulk about it.

My morning is nothing more than what I have come to expect from this week. I hover, I sit, I go on a quest to find a working CD player. After break, when I've been revived with more coffee, I'm in charge for a few minutes while Miss McCabe has to go and "sort something out". She doesn't tell me what this something is and I have no right to ask. I have very few rights here. I can't help but wonder how she would sort this mysterious thing out if I wasn't here, though. I may not be a qualified teacher but I do know leaving thirty kids alone, even for a minute, is not the done thing.

They're working on Irish worksheets, quietly filling in the blanks. Pearl hisses to the girl next to her, calling her stupid because she's filled in the wrong thing somewhere.

I go over there. "You shouldn't call people stupid." Because it's not as though Miss McCabe can get cross with me for telling her *that*, can she? Surely this is one of those things that, like saying that the sky is blue, is fairly self-evident and entirely acceptable for even the work-experience girl to pass on.

Pearl looks up at me, eyes ready to roll. After all, if I don't know my times-tables, how valid is anything that I have to say? "Why not?"

"It's rude and it hurts people's feelings."

"*Sticks and stones will break my bones but names will never hurt me!*" she chants, and then smirks.

We learned that in school too. If I was a teacher I would rip that proverb or whatever it is to shreds. Like feelings don't matter, like it's ok to be obnoxious as long as you're not beating someone up.

Now, what I should do here is explain things very calmly to Pearl and tell her that actually, names do hurt people. That being called stupid, or being called anything negative, is the sort of thing that stays with people. That words are important and do mean something, and it's not ok to throw them around. That she should respect other people's feelings and think before she speaks. That other people are actually people too, not just unfeeling beings to hurl insults at.

What actually comes out of my mouth is, in the bitchiest tone I have ever used, "Wow, I can't believe you were calling *her* stupid."

Her jaw drops.

Some part of my brain, the part that's still sane despite the exhaustion, knows that I've just done something completely inappropriate and wrong and that I've sunk to her level when I really, really should know better.

Another part of me is thrilled that she doesn't have an immediate response. I walk away.

I should care more about this. I should, but I don't.

7

Girlfriend

It starts raining just as I step outside, the kind of rain that soaks you all the way through instantly.

Fantastic. Just what I need.

It's cold, too, ice-water numbing my ears and my fingers. Why don't I ever remember my gloves? I am entirely deserving of all those dumb blonde jokes. It's the middle of winter, and my brain has yet to make the connection between the freezing cold and the need for garments that can help alleviate the chill. Idiot. I am such an idiot.

In my bag my phone's beeping. A text message. I consider checking it now, but that would mean removing my hands from where I've shoved them deep in my pockets in an attempt to keep the frostbite at bay.

I'll get back to whoever it is later. It's probably just someone else telling me they're going to the concert instead of my party, anyway. Right now all I want is to get home, and have a hot bath, and then maybe take a nap or at the very least curl up in front of the television and not think or do anything strenuous for a while.

It's so cold and miserable and horrible. I'm wearing jeans, of all things, and the wet denim is clinging to my legs, chilling them even more.

I'm turning sixteen this week and I'm supposed to be happy about this, instead of worrying about this stupid party and stupid stupid *stupid* Pearl.

I want to be happy and full of energy the way kids are, not exhausted and cranky. Is this what happens when you get older? Everything just becomes such an ordeal and nothing is fun anymore?

Is this why everyone talks about wishing they were a kid again, even though childhood isn't always that great?

Sixteen isn't really a landmark birthday. There isn't much you can do at sixteen that you can't do at fourteen or fifteen. At seventeen you can learn to drive. By eighteen you're a legal adult. You can vote and drink and all kinds of things. Not that it really changes you – I mean, Dan was eighteen back in October and he hasn't changed one bit, and Michael's turning eighteen in January and he's still, well, *Michael*

– but it's something, it's a definite step. It doesn't matter if you act grown-up or not, you *are* one, and it's not like anyone can tell you that you can't vote or something even if you are immature, because you have the right to.

Sixteen doesn't really count when you look at those things. I'm not going to have a whole bunch of extra rights once my birthday gets here. But the sound of it, the idea of it – it still feels sort of important.

It feels like I'm going to be different. Like I'm going to finally be the person that I want to be, and be the kind of teenager that I thought I'd be when I was little. Which is ridiculous, the idea that one single day is going to make such an impact, like being sixteen instead of fifteen and eleven months is going to turn me into someone completely different.

It shouldn't be this important to me. I know all of this. I know that I shouldn't be worrying about my party and about all of this, but there's knowing something intellectually and then there's feeling something, and right now it's like all I can do is feel. Feel sad and angry and upset and frustrated and tired, and I don't know how to change that. How can you control how you feel?

You can't. You can't control it.

I know that.

I still wish I could, though. It would make life a

lot easier.

When I finally get home, I pick up the post and find a card for me. From Granny. It's one of those birthday cards with a badge on it, so everyone will know how old you are.

Except I'm going to be sixteen, Granny, not fifteen.

Normally we leave cards out for everyone else to see, especially the ones from relatives, but this one I take up to my room and put in a drawer. I don't want Mum to see it and try to be nice about Granny forgetting how old I am, trying to make it funny or maybe even not noticing that it bothers me.

I know I should just be grateful that she remembered at all, or sympathetic that she's getting older and more forgetful, but all I can do is wonder why I'm the sort of person that isn't important enough to merit some kind of a reminder. Why Granny didn't phone to ask Mum if she wasn't sure, or why she didn't bother counting back the years and working it out for herself, seeing as she took care of Dan while Mum was in the hospital having me. She was *here*. Why doesn't she remember?

I opt for a shower instead of a hot bath. I'm too impatient to wait for the bath to fill up.

Besides, it's easier to cry in the shower. The hot water blasting down blocks out the sound of tears, even though no one's at home to hear me.

God, it's pathetic, isn't it? Almost sixteen and crouching in the shower sobbing like a little kid over birthday stuff.

I gulp and I gasp and I turn my face up to the water and let it wash everything away, and now that I'm home and don't have to do anything apart from sit around in my dressing-gown for the rest of the evening, I feel a little better.

Which is when the doorbell rings. I curse loudly and decide that if it's anyone looking for money for any reason, even if it's for charity, I will shut the door in their face.

I have a towel on my head and am wearing a pink fluffy dressing-gown and mismatched slippers – actually, one slipper and one slipper sock. Eddie laughs when he sees me.

"What are you doing here?" I ask. I pause and note the smile on his face disappearing. "I didn't mean it like that," I say, leaning over to kiss him. "I'm just surprised."

"I sent you a text," he says, coming in and dumping his school bag on the floor.

"Oh. Oh, right. I haven't checked my phone yet. I got soaked on the way home, so I just went straight into the shower."

"Yeah, I noticed," he smiles, and moves in to kiss me again. We stay like that for a while, but I'm very conscious that I'm in nothing but a dressing-gown and a towel, and that the front hall is not really the sort of place where I want to be close to naked with Eddie.

We haven't really ventured that far into naked territory. Actually, naked territory is an entirely separate country to where Eddie and I are. I think it'll probably happen after we cross the one-year anniversary line. Not that we've really talked about it, but he's said that the one-year thing is a big deal. Euphemisms like "the next level" and "a big step" have been thrown around a bit.

I don't know why I haven't just asked him about it directly. I guess it's just that it's a relief, in some ways, to have Eddie be so unlike the boys like Tom who spend all their time pushing for sex to happen, who are more concerned with getting their girlfriends into bed than establishing a relationship. It's nice.

I mean, why would I force a conversation about something I'm not even sure I want to happen, anyway?

"I'm going to go and put some clothes on," I say. "Do you want coffee or anything?"

"No, I'm ok."

I go upstairs and get dressed. I leave my hair wet but take it out of the towel and comb it out, and spray on a bit of perfume before I return to Eddie.

We sit on the couch and have the TV switched on

while he tells me about his day, and I nod and smile and reply and keep one eye on the sitcom they're repeating in the afternoons.

"How are you doing? Did you get to sleep last night?"

"Yeah, I'm fine, everything's ok," I say, and of course it's a blatant lie but the truth is that I don't want to explain things to Eddie. Or I can't. Or – I don't want to think about it.

I kiss him instead, because at least then he can't ask me questions and I don't have to lie.

8

Friend

After Eddie leaves – he has his fencing class on Thursday evenings – I'm past the point of being able to take a nap and still sleep tonight, which annoys me.

It doesn't have anything to do with him. Just that I'm tired, that's all. I need to remember that. I need to not be an irrational girlfriend who takes out all her problems on her boyfriend. I need to be sensible and calm.

I check my phone and there's the message from him saying that he's going to come over unless I have any objections. The beeping I ignored earlier because I was cold and tired.

Isn't it generally considered more polite to ask instead of tell someone, or at the very least to wait for a response? I could have been busy. I could have been out of the house. I could have had plans that didn't involve being available for him to see.

Once my party's over and done with, it'll all be ok, I tell myself. I'm just a little stressed out right now. I shouldn't get annoyed with Eddie.

I'm crazy about him. I mean, why else would we have stayed together for nearly a year? I'm not like Dawn, unable to go more than a week without a boy at my side. I want this.

I sit with my laptop on my knees and listen to the songs on the birthday playlist while checking my email.

I'm deleting a whole selection of spam offering me Viagra and imitations of Swiss watches when the second song comes on. It's this fun little bouncy tune called 'My Dream Boy' that was a summer hit back when I was eleven or twelve. I loved it so much. I hadn't ever had a boyfriend then but the song inspired images of the perfect guy for me, sweet and sensitive and funny and charming, and I sang along to it passionately whenever it was on the radio or TV, like my own rendition of the lyrics would produce my own dream boy right before my eyes. Dan mocked me mercilessly and left the room whenever the song came on, but Michael would hang around if the video was shown on TV – supposedly to lecture me on my bad taste, but really to appreciate the fine dancing of one of the band members, a particularly attractive and well-endowed redheaded girl. It was an embarrassing infatuation – as someone who was against the idea of manufactured music and bands, he should've been ogling someone with principles or, at the very least, a better sense of rhythm. We had a deal going whereby he wouldn't mock my fondness for that particular song if I wouldn't tease him for having a crush on someone who had 'sold out'.

It was one of the first times Michael and I had something that was just ours. I think it was around that summer when he stopped being 'Dan's friend Michael' and started being just Michael.

I'm smiling as I listen to it. I still know all the words, still remember the dance, can still see Michael's redhead roll her shoulders forward and wink at the camera.

There's an email from him, one of those forwarded lists where you mark off the things that you've done in your lifetime, like shoplifted or kissed someone of the same sex or visited all seven continents or gone swimming with dolphins. I skim through, already knowing that his 'yes' answer to shoplifting involves nothing more exotic than a packet of Smarties, how the picture of his photocopied rear end turned out, and that at least one of the times he took care of a drunk person involves that time about a year and a half ago when I was very very ill at a small but alcohol-laden get-together he had at his house.

Seeing a 'yes' answer to the ones about having your heart broken or having cried yourself to sleep makes me feel very strange, though, like something's shifted. I know these things about Eddie, know how upset he was after Laura dumped him, but knowing them about Michael feels like too much. It's too personal, too private, too intimate.

I mean, I know that breaking up with Caitriona was rough on him. I just didn't know that he considered his heart *broken* by the experience, that he had cried that much over her. When they were going out, he complained about her more than he praised her. I always figured that anyone who had that many bad things to say about someone couldn't possibly really care about them.

It's always easier to judge when you're looking in from the outside.

I suddenly feel protective of him, wanting to hug him and make everything ok, even though he'd probably laugh if I tried. Anyway, it's all past tense – just because he's had his heart broken in the past doesn't mean that he's still heartbroken over it. It's been – how long? Six months, maybe longer. The time to hug him about it would have been right after they broke up, except when he told me he said it so matter-of-factly that I assumed he really was as ok with it as he seemed.

I should have known. I should have known that he was really upset about it, should have been there to stroke his hair or something. He was there for me after Tom and I broke up. He was there with coffee. I should have been able to do that for him.

The fourth song on the playlist is the one that was playing at the New Year's Eve party right about when I decided that this guy Eddie that I was talking to was the one for me.

I skip to the next one.

The computer chimes to tell me I have an instant message from Elaine, who's currently signed in as Pretentious Artsy Chick. We chat for a bit. She doesn't bring up Michael, which – considering she's the one who, not three weeks ago, suggested that maybe he was attracted to me – is completely inconsiderate of her. You don't just say something like that to someone and then fail to dissect it at the next available opportunity.

Of course, I can't bring it up. If I bring it up, it will completely undermine my no-you're-crazy-let's-move-on stance.

Obviously, I'm not interested in him. Because I have a boyfriend. And I can look terrible in front of Michael and not worry about it. And I've known him for far too long. It's just – I suppose it's just that whenever you find out that someone you respect and care about might be into you in that way, it's sort of flattering. Thinking about it and liking the idea of it doesn't mean that you like someone back.

Because of course it'd be really flattering to have Michael like me in that way, when he knows me so well that there'd be very little mystery, when he's nearly two years older than me and nearly an actual adult.

I mean, it'd be a sign that he no longer sees me as that stupid little girl who needs to have her head held as she throws up from drinking too much, or that silly kid who followed him and Dan around when they were out having their 'adventures' (mostly pretending to be pirates) in the local park.

I'm not a child any more. It'd be nice if someone, someone who knew me as a child instead of only knowing the teenage-Kim, could recognise that.

That's what it's all about, I decide.

I turn my attention fully to Elaine's account of running into her ex-boyfriend Julian the other day, who went on and on about his new girlfriend in a blatant attempt to make her jealous.

* * *

Pretentious Artsy Chick says: **It was so obvious that he just wanted me to throw myself at his feet and beg for him to take me back.**

Kimperfection says: **Ugh. What did you do?**

Pretentious Artsy Chick says: **Told him I was very happy for him and then got the hell out of there.**

Kimperfection says: **Sensible girl. Proud of you!**

Pretentious Artsy Chick says: **Yeah . . . for a very brief second I wanted to, though. Not throw myself, but . . . I know that if I said to him that I wanted to get back with him, he would do it right away.**

Kimperfection says: **You just like the power over him!**

Pretentious Artsy Chick says: **Yeah, kinda. Well... I do miss him sometimes. I mean, I still like him, even though I know it's never going to work out and we're better off like this. And I wish I didn't. AAAAAAGH!**

Kimperfection says: **You can't control how you feel, though.**

Pretentious Artsy Chick says: **I know. One of the great tragedies of life.**

Kimperfection says: **Really is.**

9

Daughter

Some days you wake up and the world seems brighter. Today is one of them.

This is possibly because I got a full night's sleep last night. And because today's my last day of work experience. And it's Friday, which is always a positive thing even if tomorrow is the day of the party.

Don't think about it, I chastise myself as I walk to St Joseph's. Don't worry about it. Worrying is pointless, remember?

I run into Allie Carter, who has a four-year-old and an eight-year-old in the school. She's a friend of Mum's; I baby-sit the kids sometimes.

"Hi, Kim! What are you doing up around these parts?"

"I'm on work experience this week," I say.

"Oh, really? How are you finding it?"

"It's ok." Apart from Pearl. And spending more time hovering than doing anything useful. And being tired all the time. But today is Friday and that's all that matters.

"Sure, it'd be no problem for you, they're lucky to have you. Listen, pet, are you around the weekend after next? I have to work Saturday afternoon and I need someone to be there with the girls."

"Yeah, that sounds fine," I nod.

"Grand, I'll give you a ring sometime during the week with the details. Listen, have a brilliant birthday, and tell your mum and Jim hello from me, ok?"

I walk into the classroom smiling. I like Allie's kids, and it's nice to have a reminder that I'm not always this useless and helpless, that there are kids out there who do think I'm cool and fun to have around.

It's just that I'm not really needed here. But that's fine, because by the end of today I'll be finished and I won't need to think about this class ever again. Just another few hours and it's all over.

That knowledge doesn't make the day go any faster, but it does make it less frustrating.

I pull Pearl aside at break-time and say, "I'm sorry for what I said to you yesterday. I shouldn't have said that."

I am mature. I am going to be turning sixteen in two days. I am able to recognise when I have done something wrong and apologise for it.

She wrinkles up her nose and shrugs. "Whatever," she says, and walks off to go talk to her friends.

I still want to strangle her.

When the final bell of the day rings, Miss McCabe thanks me half-heartedly for my help throughout the week, and I smile with relief that it's over.

Walking out, I see that Pearl's mum has come to the school door to collect her and Pearl's glaring at her for not staying well out of sight.

I remember being ten and Mum not trusting me to make it from the classroom to her car (though in fairness this was after a few incidents in which I'd deliberately wandered off on my own for a couple of hours, so it wasn't entirely unjustified) and how embarrassing it was to be treated like a baby.

I smile sympathetically at Pearl as I pass by. She just sticks her tongue out at me.

I hope I never, ever have a child like her.

At least she's honest about how she feels about people, the optimist in me pipes up. It's just my misfortune to be disliked by her.

It's so easy for kids to tell people that they don't like them. It's so straightforward and simple – harsh and horrible a lot of the time, but at least it's clear-cut.

When you're little you have your friends and your enemies and you know exactly who's who.

Then you grow up, and it gets complicated.

* * *

Dad and Annelise pick me up at five and take me out to dinner in honour of my birthday. We once tried being very sensible and reasonable about everything and had the whole family there for Dan's seventeenth birthday, with Mum and Jim and Dad and Annelise, but it was painfully civil instead of being fun, and then Dan walked out halfway through, so we went back to separate celebrations.

Annelise is this classic Mediterranean beauty with a completely incongruous Donegal accent. I like her because of that and because she's sweet and interested in what I have to say, but not overly so. Dad's first post-break-up 'lady friend' was this simpering idiot who cooed over me and so clearly wanted me to think of her as a second mother that it was sickening. Annelise has no such illusions.

"How's school going?" Dad asks.

"Ok," I reply.

"Have any exams coming up?"

"No, it's Transition Year," I remind him.

"Do you not do exams in Transition Year?"

I shake my head and know that I've explained it all before.

"It's continuous assessment and project work and all that, Sam," Annelise says, stepping in. "It's not a set curriculum. Have you had work experience yet, Kim?"

Another thing I like about Annelise: she has never, ever tried calling me Kimmie.

"Yeah, just finished this week. I was in the primary school over near the shopping centre, with fifth class."

"Oh, that's St Joseph's, isn't it?"

I nod. "It was all right, kind of boring. I don't know if I'd want to go into teaching, but it's hard to tell, because it's only a week and you don't really get to do anything interesting with them, you know?"

"Sure, sure, it's hard when you're just there for a short while. You can't really know what it's like from that," she nods.

"It'd be a good job to have, though," Dad says. "Three years for the degree and you're set for life. You should think about it."

"I will," I say quietly.

"Plenty of time for that, anyway," Annelise says brightly. "How's Dan doing filling out his CAO form, Kim?"

"It's a work in progress," I say diplomatically.

"I don't know why he won't just put down

medicine," Dad says. "He'd be brilliant at it."

"Medicine's hard to get into," I say, shamelessly plagiarising another of Dan's favourite rants, College Courses That Are Impossible To Get Into Unless You Have Been Cramming Since Age Four.

"He has the brains for it, it's not a problem," Dad says.

"Yeah, but it's a really tough exam, Dad. I mean, you only get one shot at it, and there's so much pressure on people to do well, and I don't know if he even *wants* to do medicine, anyway." (Some of this material is taken from Dan's Why Continuous Assessment Should Be Introduced As The Pressure Caused By Just Having One Set Of Exams Is Eventually Going To Make The Universe Implode tirade.)

"It'd be a pity if he doesn't. Waste of his talents," Dad sighs.

"He'll figure out what he wants to do," I say, even though I'm not entirely sure of this myself. I think it's entirely possible he'll spontaneously combust from trying to decide what he wants.

It's just that whenever things get like this, it turns into kids-versus-parents and I have to be on Dan's team, even if I see Dad's point. I mean, it's ok for me to criticise Dan. But Dad hasn't spent enough time with him in the last couple of years to be able to do that. He's lost that privilege.

"Sure he will," Annelise says. "Now, come on, what are you going to get?"

She talks about her work and her four-year-old nephew while we're waiting for our starters. I'm two mouthfuls into my melon when Dad manages to drive the conversation back to people using their potential and why it's deeply tragic if they don't, and even though he's talking in the abstract it's painfully obvious that this is yet another rendition of What Dan Should Do With His Life.

I order something chocolate-heavy from the dessert menu that is described as 'sinful', and think about people who have families who arrange for birthday cakes to be delivered to their table, and for waiters to sing to the birthday girl or boy in question. Not that I want that, particularly.

It's just that this is supposed to be a celebration, and I'm fairly sure that this evening couldn't be reasonably described as 'festive' under any definition of the word.

The chocolate concoction is pretty good, though.

10

Ostrich

"It's just a stupid question. Look at it. I mean, how is that related to chemistry? *How?* Why the hell should we have to answer stuff like that, huh? It's just –"

"Completely unreasonable," I say, finishing off Dan's rant for him.

Dan and Michael are spending their Friday night in the study, surrounded by textbooks and sets of past exam papers. How very hip and groovy of them.

They're on opposite ends of the couch, like two strangers sharing a seat on the bus. Boys. Honestly. I sit down between them and turn to Dan. "You should have come to dinner."

"Why?" He's instantly hostile.

"Because all Dad ever does is talk about you," I say.

"Just – give him a call soon, ok?"

"It's none of your business," he growls, and his phone starts buzzing. "It's Saoirse," he says, answering it as he walks out of the room.

"You shouldn't push him, Kimmie," Michael says.

I turn around to look at him and glare. "I just spent *my* birthday dinner talking about Dan, ok? Do you even – oh, forget it. You don't get it."

I slam the door on my way out.

I hate it when Michael takes Dan's side in things. He doesn't even know what he's talking about.

Five minutes later I'm back in the study. "Hey. I'm sorry. I shouldn't have snapped at you like that."

Michael's still alone, a finger marking his place in *Othello*. "It's ok. I shouldn't have said anything."

There's an awkward silence and I look at my shoes for a while before saying, "Is Dan still talking to Saoirse?"

"Yep."

I sit down next to him. "I hate it when people do that."

"What?"

"Forget about their friends when there's a romantic interest thing going on."

"You're such a girl," he says.

"Oh, come on. Don't tell me it doesn't bother you that any time a girl's into him, he forgets about anything else."

"He likes her," Michael shrugs.

"It's ok to have feelings, Mikey," I say. And to actually share them with people who care. Hint hint.

"Give it a rest, Kim, would you?"

"Fine."

But it's a comfortable silence this time; he's not really annoyed with me.

I can feel his right leg against my left. It's warm. I freeze, afraid that if I move even just a little, he'll shift away from me.

Then I come to my senses and realise that it's Michael. It's not like it's the first time we've ever touched. We've slept in the same bed; I've sat on his knee or leaned against him more times than I can count. Physical contact with Michael isn't unusual. It's everyday.

It doesn't matter whether his leg is against mine or not, even if it is tingle-inducing.

"I'll see you later," I say, getting up.

He nods in acknowledgement.

Up in my room I put on some music, a new CD with no history yet, no stories attached.

It's just because of what Elaine said. It's just the thought of Michael as someone who might actually like me that's throwing everything off-course like this, it's just me reacting to that and nothing more. It's me adapting and absorbing new information, which I'm going to dismiss anyway, because of course he doesn't like me.

Of course he doesn't.

He couldn't.

And it doesn't even matter. Why am I thinking about this? Why am I wasting my time worrying about it?

Let go, let go, I tell myself. Let go.

My room feels too small. I turn on the computer and check my email compulsively. Spam, spam, a few newsletters from music websites announcing new releases. I delete once I'm finished and I'm back again at Michael's life-experience list.

I read through it again, slowly and carefully, as though it's a carefully crafted memoir instead of the kind of thing people spend five minutes filling out when they're bored or procrastinating. He's cried himself to sleep. He's had his heart broken. He can't talk about how it feels when his best friend abandons him because of a girl but he can share these kinds of things via email.

I shouldn't be thinking about Michael this much.

Eddie. Eddie is my boyfriend. Think about Eddie.

In a few weeks we'll have been together for an entire year. It's not quite as crazily long-term as those couples who get together at thirteen or something and spend their entire teenage years as part of a unit, but it's – a year. A whole year of my life, with this boy that I think I love.

I used to be surer of that. Dawn and Bonnie and Mandy and people like that, they fall in love immediately. Two weeks into a relationship and they're ready to tell everyone – even if not the boy in question – how in love they are. Dawn practically has her whole wedding planned out by the time she gets to the three-week stage.

I remember Truth or Dare in the Gaeltacht, the secrets emerging in the dark. I was asked if I'd ever been in love. It was an easy question to answer. (I later found out, via Elaine, that the only reason Richard had asked me such a non-scandalous question was because he was hoping I was secretly in love with him, being somewhat out of the loop when it came to knowing who had a significant other at home.) Yes. Yes, I had been in love. I was in love. I did love somebody.

There was a disco on the last night that all the other girls, the awful ones I was sharing a room with and the lovely ones that I'd got to know throughout the course, were looking forward to. It was the only real chance to dress up and wear make-up and make a move on whichever boy they'd been eyeing up for the last couple of weeks. They even let us have proper music despite the lyrics not being in Irish.

Three of us – myself, Elaine, and another girl, Jessica – banded together for the night. We all had boyfriends at home – Elaine was still with Julian then – and unlike some of the girls there, we didn't think that being a couple of hundred miles away from home meant that cheating was suddenly magically ok.

"D'you ever wish that you were single and could just – do whatever you liked with anyone?" Jessica asked us.

Dawn had asked me pretty much the same question a month or two before, looking for someone to sympathise with her perpetual plight. The funny thing was that I'd said to her that I could see her point, that yeah, there was a downside to being in a relationship.

With Jessica, away from everyone at school and everyone at home, I was honest. "No," I said. "I'm not interested in anyone except Eddie."

"There's no point in being with someone if you'd rather be off scoring every random guy in sight," Elaine pointed out.

We watched Cara, one of Jessica's roommates, all done up in glitter and fake tan, drape her arms around some guy's neck. I wondered what she was talking to him about, what side of herself she was showing off so that he'd like her. I didn't envy her and the others, in the early stages of excitement and hope and anxiety and promise. It was a fun stage to be in, but I didn't miss it. I didn't desperately want to be among them again. What I had with Eddie was enough.

I agreed with Elaine – what was the point of having a boyfriend if you kept craving that initial thrill of the chase? Either you wanted to be with someone or you didn't, and there was no middle ground.

I still believe that. Don't I?

I have a party tomorrow night. Now isn't the time to make important decisions. I'm not thinking clearly, I'm not being rational. I just need – to sleep. To get some rest and get through tomorrow and not worry about any of the thoughts dancing around inside my brain.

Everything will be ok once the party is over. Everything will be ok once I turn sixteen and get back to my normal life.

Everything is going to be fine.

and promised I'd [illegible] to be [illegible] I didn't miss [illegible] desperately [illegible] to be among them again. What I had with Charlie was enough.

I agreed with [illegible] – what was the point of having [illegible] that [illegible] the chance [illegible] you wanted to be with someone or you didn't, and there was no middle ground.

I still believe that. Don't I?

[illegible] party tomorrow night. Now isn't the time to make important [illegible] I'm not thinking clearly. I'm not being rational. I just need – to sleep, to get some rest and get through tomorrow, and not worry about any of the thoughts [illegible]

[illegible] everything will be [illegible] the party [illegible]

[illegible] it's going to be fine.

A Sunday [illegible]

[illegible]

everyone [illegible]

friends [illegible]

So it's [illegible]

wrong [illegible]

[illegible]

I can't [illegible]

11

Hostess

In less than twenty-four hours I'm going to be sixteen.

It's tempting fate to celebrate today, I think as I lie in bed on Saturday morning. I'm not sixteen yet. This evening people are going to wish me a happy birthday and it's going to be meaningless.

A Sunday birthday means you can celebrate a day or two early or five or six days late, and next weekend is far too close to Christmas to have a party – everyone's doing things with family rather than friends; we normally have something on that weekend too. So it's a day early, and suddenly that feels so off and wrong. It's counting your chickens before they've hatched and all that.

I can't believe I'm worrying about tempting fate. I

mean, I don't even believe in fate, or destiny, or any of that rubbish. That stuff belongs in fantasy books, or really horrendously trashy romance novels, not in real life.

I spend my morning tidying the house. I am a fairly clean, organised person. In theory. I mean, I would never leave plates of food or dirty socks or anything lying around on the floor of my bedroom, because that's just disgusting. But I have bits of paper and magazines and books and CDs everywhere on the floor. It's a clean kind of chaos, and I always intend to sort it out. I just don't ever seem to get around to it.

I drag out the vacuum cleaner, inspiring Jim to make a very feeble joke about how I should have parties more often if this is what it leads to.

He's not the world's greatest comic genius. Not by a long shot. In fact, the funniest thing he's ever said was at last year's Christmas party when he told us that he sometimes thought about leaving his job to try to make it as a stand-up comedian. That, unfortunately, wasn't meant to be laughed at.

When all the carpets are free of dirt and anything else that might be lurking within their depths, I move on to dusting, then to cleaning the windows, then to putting CDs and DVDs back in their cases, which go back in their racks. In alphabetical order. I contemplate putting all the breakables – all the fiddly little ornaments sitting on the mantelpiece, for example – away, but I decide that if I was at a house where someone else's parents were looming over everything, I probably wouldn't even pick up anything that looked delicate, let alone play with it to the extent that it could break. This is not going to be the kind of wild party where valuables get broken. This is going to be the kind of party where hand-eye co-ordination will be maintained, not destroyed.

Elaine, Eddie and Bonnie are coming over for six. The party starts at seven.

It is now two o'clock, and the house is cleaner than it has ever been, even cleaner than when Mum went on her crazy cleaning spree right after Dad moved out.

I check my email a dozen times and then flop in front of the television, watching the second half of an episode of *Friends* that has been shown approximately ten million times before.

It's two-thirty.

I just want this whole thing to be over with. Done. Finished. In the past. It feels like something to get through instead of something to look forward to and enjoy, and I hate that it feels like that.

It's my party, and my birthday, and I shouldn't feel like this. I don't want to feel like this.

At around three o'clock Dan emerges from his room and asks my opinion on a shirt.

"It's fine," I say, as though there's any real difference between that shirt and all the others that he wears. All dark colours, all looking fairly identical to my eye. He has yet to discover colours that fall outside of the blue/black spectrum. "Are you wearing that tonight?"

"Yeah, I'm going out with Saoirse."

"What?"

"I said I'm going out with Saoirse," he repeats.

"I heard you, I just – did you forget something? The something that we're having here, in this very house, tonight?"

"Oh, come on, Kim, it's not like you'll even notice I'm not here. It's your thing, not mine. And I really want to see Saoirse tonight."

He retreats back into his room and leaves me speechless. He doesn't even see this as a big deal. It's more important that he go out with his new girlfriend than be there for his sister's birthday. How could anyone expect his priorities to be different?

Silly, silly me, how could I ever think that anyone would ever put me first on the one day of the year that I need them to?

I make a beeline for the shower so that I can cry without anyone hearing me.

By six o'clock I am even cleaner than the house, rinsed and purified of all impurities, in theory anyway. I put on my favourite, hardly-worn red dress and stare at myself in the mirror. Today, I hate how I look. The dress feels too formal, too uncomfortable, and I end up in a black outfit, a silky top and smart trousers, safe and boring.

At two minutes past six Elaine arrives, in a very classy dark purple dress that makes me feel completely lacking in style, and thirty seconds later I see Bonnie approaching, wearing a very very very short skirt. She looks a hundred thousand times more confident and sure of herself than I am.

And then there's Eddie, all tall and sandy-haired and smiling, with a bouquet of roses and a box of chocolates for his lady love.

"Thank you," I say, and smile back, and notice that Bonnie and Elaine are already bonding by being the ones left out of this romantic display.

I'm kissing Eddie and I can hear them, play-acting, Bonnie pretending to be distraught that no one has ever given her roses and Elaine pretending to despair at the state of the universe, and I know that I didn't need to worry about whether they'd get along.

Perhaps what I should have been worrying about is the fact that kissing Eddie feels like an obligation, a duty instead of a pleasure.

Roses. Roses and chocolates. It's all so very romantic. I should be considering myself lucky to have a boyfriend who gives me roses and chocolates.

But. Well. When Eddie turned sixteen two months ago I picked out things I thought he'd like. I asked one of his friends for advice, even though I don't know any of them that well. I thoroughly examined his CD collection and bookshelves to make sure that I wasn't going to get him something that he already had.

Birthday presents, all presents, really, are supposed to be uniquely tailored to the individual. At least that's what I think, but I don't consider this a particularly revolutionary perspective on the whole gift-giving matter.

I have never in my life expressed an appreciation of roses. And, ok, sure, I like chocolates, but who doesn't like chocolates? Eddie himself is not a chocoholic but has still been known to consume the stuff when it's around. Boxes of chocolates are what you buy for people when you're not sure what to get them. They're risk-free – it's not as though anyone minds having duplicates when it comes to chocolates. The absolute worst-case scenario is that the box is left out for guests to help themselves to when they come over, because someone's on a diet or has a nut allergy or something. Chocolates are completely and utterly safe.

Flowers and a box of chocolates. The ideal present for every girl, for any girl, and requiring no thought whatsoever.

Once Eddie and I separate, because it's incredibly rude to stay glued to your boyfriend's lips when you have company, and also because I really need some space, Bonnie gives me her gift.

It's a DVD of a Lucy Marshall concert, which I've been eying in HMV for ages but never actually got around to buying, even though I love Lucy Marshall (despite Michael's assertion that she's whiny and her lyrics are unremarkable and uninspired and that she can't play the guitar as well as his idols – all male – can).

I am much more thankful for this than I am for the roses. Which might make me something of an ingrate, but I don't care because it's my birthday and my boyfriend opted for something completely clichéd instead of something thoughtful and my brother's out with some girl instead of being here and two of my best friends look more beautiful than I will ever look and it's my *birthday*, for God's sake, and doesn't that mean anything anymore?

"Thank you so much!" I say to Bonnie, who beams.

"I do have something for you," Elaine puts in, "but it's not quite ready – you'll have to wait until later."

I grin. "I'm intrigued."

She laughs.

Mum and Jim emerge from the kitchen. "Hi, everyone," Mum says, nodding to Eddie, then Bonnie, then Elaine. Jim shakes Eddie's hand. This is something he seems to do whenever Eddie is around. I have no idea why. It's not as though Jim is my dad, needing to establish himself as the primary male figure in my life or anything like that. I hope that's not why he does it.

"We've set out all the drinks and the food inside," Mum says, gesturing in the direction of the sitting room, which opens out into a conservatory-type structure that took about two years of builders traipsing through the house and using up all the coffee to actually finish. I'm glad we have it, but I'm not sure it was worth two years.

Eddie heads directly for the food, helping himself to a couple of cocktail sausages. Bonnie, Elaine and I all look at each other and smile. Typical boy behaviour. Food first.

Elaine has brought decorations, hand-crafted paper things that need to be pinned up. Eddie offers to help, and Bonnie and I go upstairs to my room, telling them to follow us when they're done.

Bonnie has brought her extensive hair-care-product collection over to ensure that my hair doesn't look entirely vile tonight.

"Why aren't you wearing the red?" she asks as she expertly curls my hair, seeing the dress lying over the end of my bed.

I shrug. "It just didn't look that great on me," I say.

"Red really suits you, though. Pity." She pauses. "Plus, it'd match your roses."

I giggle. So does she.

"I can't believe he got you *roses.* I mean, it's really sweet, but –"

"But I'm not really the roses type?"

"Yeah. I mean, they must have cost him a fortune and all, but it's not really your thing, is it?"

"It's Eddie's thing, though," I say, and we're both quiet for a moment. Even talking like this feels disloyal. And dangerous.

"Elaine's nice," Bonnie says. "Those decorations are gorgeous."

I nod, which messes up the handful of hair that's being curled at the moment. Bonnie has to redo it.

I hear footsteps coming up the stairs. Eddie has only been in my room a couple of times. Firstly because Mum and Jim have their policy about keeping young men downstairs so as not to impregnate me, or whatever they think is going to happen, and secondly because it's usually so messy that I keep him out of it. Just because it's only a paper sort of mess doesn't mean I think it's a good idea to show it off.

It's like taking your clothes off or something, to let people into your bedroom. I feel exposed with Eddie here, especially because this is really the first time he's ever been able to look around properly, the first time he's been in here without having all of his attention focussed on kissing me.

With Elaine and Bonnie it's different, because they know all the secrets of girls' bedrooms already. Or maybe it's not the difference between girls and boys but the one between friends and boyfriends that matters.

Eddie is examining my teddy collection. Teddy bears, not lingerie, that is. A few are from when I was a kid, others are more recent gifts. The green one with KIM on it was from Bonnie on my thirteenth birthday. The red one with a tartan ribbon around its neck and surprisingly soft fur was from Michael the Christmas before last. The koala was a present from Deirdre, bought when she was in Australia last year.

I can't tell what he thinks, whether he thinks it's childish to still keep teddy bears in your bedroom at almost-sixteen, or whether he gets it, that it's about wanting to have things that remind you of people you care about.

My phone beeps and if it's someone saying that they can't come I think I'll cry. But it's Jessica from the Gaeltacht, and it's a last-minute request for the address because it turns out she's actually up in Dublin this weekend instead of at home in Waterford as per usual.

"Jessica's coming," I tell Elaine.

Her face lights up. "Brilliant! I haven't seen her in ages."

"Gaeltacht person?" Bonnie asks, arranging my newly curled hair so that some of the curls fall down on either side of my face and some are pinned up. I answer yes into a cloud of hairspray.

Eddie looks on in wonder. "So that's how hairspray works," he says, as though the secrets of the universe have been uncovered.

"Yes. It's a miracle," Bonnie laughs.

The person in the mirror is almost pretty. She has pretty hair, at any rate. I don't want to obsess. I just want to have a good time tonight. Jessica's going to be here, that's good news, even if it doesn't compensate for Dan not caring or Dawn not even noticing or Orla not bothering.

It's nearly seven. Funny how time slows down and then speeds up on you.

Most of my friends are of the seven-means-seven-thirty variety. The ones who fall into the camp of always being on time are the ones who are here already.

"Let's head downstairs," I suggest, and down we go. Mum and Jim are admiring the decorations and double-checking the Coke supply.

I put on the music and note Eddie's arms around

my waist. He's telling me I look beautiful and I can't concentrate because I'm thinking of how I need to be a good hostess and not just wrapped up in my boyfriend, and also because I don't believe him.

I can't breathe.

"Eddie," I say, pushing him away, "can we – not – I mean, the parents are around, you know?"

He frowns a little but then says, "Ok. Yeah. I know."

I smile and try to make it all better. I'm not sure it's working. And then the doorbell rings, and it's Deirdre, and then Susan from down the road with her boyfriend, and then a whole bunch of Eddie's friends, and I'm taking coats and directing people into the sitting room and smiling and accepting the birthday wishes even though it's not really my birthday yet, and I'm the hostess and it's happening. It's here, the party is really here.

12

Party Girl

The party-induced panic has lifted somewhat, maybe because there's a whole load of people here and they're having fun and everything's ok and the worries seem silly now, maybe because I've moved on to worrying about this odd feeling concerning Eddie, this sense that we don't fit together.

"Oh my God, those roses are gorgeous," Deirdre says to me. "Did Eddie get you those?"

"Yeah," I say, and smile, because that's what I'm supposed to do. That's what you're supposed to do when your boyfriend gets you flowers. I'm a lucky girl, right?

I think nearly everyone is here now. Jim is talking to Eddie and a few of his friends about football, or maybe it's football-related computer games. Susan and her boyfriend are talking to Mandy and her boyfriend over by the door, with the rest of the primary school crowd hovering nearby. Bonnie, Deirdre and I are next to the food, nibbling on teeny-tiny crackers shaped like fish, and Jessica and Elaine are catching up on Gaeltacht-related scandal nearby. (Richard and Cara apparently hooked up a while back when they ran into each other at a party, even though Cara is, as far as we know, still seeing the guy she was with on the last night. Jessica's ability to keep up with what people have been doing is impressive. I've been getting emails from the Gaeltacht people too but I had no idea about half of this stuff.) There's a couple more girls from school due to arrive, and then Michael, and I think that's it.

Unless of course Michael's decided not to bother coming because at the end of the day he's still really Dan's friend and not mine, and if Dan's not here then there's no reason for him to be.

I still can't quite believe Dan is out with his girlfriend instead of at his sister's birthday party. Except that I don't know why it surprises me, because he's always picked girls over friends or family, as though he's afraid that if he doesn't make them his number one priority he'll be alone forever.

Don't think about it, I tell myself. Just have fun.

Enjoy the party. Enjoy that people are talking to one another and that there have been no complaints about the music and that, even though Mum and Jim are around instead of making themselves absent, it's going well.

"Kim!" Elaine is beckoning me over to where she and Jessica are sitting, perched on the chairs that have been pushed back against the wall so that there's room for dancing, or at the very least swaying while chatting.

"Julian's here," she announces as I sit down next to them.

"Julian? What!" My eyes widen. "Which one is he?" Eddie must have invited him. I try to remember if Eddie knows a Julian, but Elaine is pointing – surreptitiously – over in the direction of the door.

"The one in the black," she says. "With the girl with the red hair."

"That's Mandy. I didn't know, Elaine." Mandy didn't introduce us. I've given up on trying to remember her boyfriends' names, anyway.

"He is cute," Jessica says.

"Yeah," Elaine nods. "I can't believe he's here."

"Have you said hi?" I ask.

"No, I don't think he's noticed me yet. I don't even know if I want him to. It might be better if we just avoid each other." She looks tense.

I squeeze her hand. "It'll be ok," I say.

"Yeah. There's plenty of people here. You don't have to talk to him if you don't want to," Jessica adds.

"Right," Elaine says quietly, and sighs. "Ok. It'll be fine. Hey, is Michael here yet?"

"I haven't seen him," I say. I wait for her to say more, to remind us both of the suggestion that he might like me, so that I can get her to elaborate on the whole thing instead of just dismissing it, but she doesn't.

I wander over to Mandy's cluster of people, who are migrating outside en masse in order to get their nicotine fix. I position myself so that I avoid most of the smoke and talk to Niamh, who was my best friend back in junior infants. That fact is probably the only reason we're still in touch. She goes to this posh secondary school that's an hour away and is supposed to be brilliant, but as far as academics go she doesn't seem to be doing all that well. I think the only thing they really teach there is superficiality. She has turned into one of those people who spend hundreds of euro on designer handbags. I try to be enthusiastic about her latest one, which she proudly displays, but I keep thinking about all the CDs you could buy with that amount of money instead.

We get talking about primary school and Mandy joins in and says, "Oh, Kim, remember that time when we were doing art and you poured the dirty water all over the teacher? What was her name again?"

"Mandy, don't," I say sharply even as people are shrieking and going, "Really? Kim did that?"

"Oh, come on, Kim, it's funny," she laughs. "Our teacher, whatever her name was, she tells Kim that she's done something the wrong colour or something, so Kim turns around, gets the jar – you know, the jars you have with water for cleaning off the brushes – and empties it out all over the teacher's shoes, then smashes it on the ground and storms off. Can you imagine Kim doing something like that?"

Funny, I can, right now, with that glass of Club Orange she's holding. I can easily imagine ruining her shoes, breaking glass, running away in anger.

I'm sure it's an amusing image if you're used to a Kim who's normally calm and would never do a thing like that, but it's really not all that hilarious if you've asked someone not to tell a story like that and they have anyway.

But then again Mandy never listens to anyone unless they're telling her what she wants to hear. It's more important for her to get to tell her stories than to be considerate of people's feelings. Maybe next she can tell the story about the screaming match I had with Mum in the car park one day after school. That would be nice and sensitive of her.

I raise an eyebrow at her, and then I go back inside.

I'm a big girl now. In a few hours I'll be sixteen years old, too old to throw a temper tantrum, too old to smash things, too old to yell and scream at Mandy for doing exactly the sort of thing I didn't want anyone doing, telling embarrassing stories about me from primary school, especially ones from the time Mum and Dad were splitting up.

So I just breathe and try to relax. Jessica and Elaine have moved from their chairs. I find Jessica in the kitchen talking to a few of the girls from school, including Carrie, who has just arrived, and looking at the picture of me, Dan and Michael up on the wall.

"Aw, Kim, you look so cute!" Carrie grins.

I'm so used to the picture that I haven't properly looked at it in ages, but I know that it's obligatory to say that kids, especially if they're younger versions of someone you know, look adorable in photos. I look at the Michael on the wall, and wonder if the two-dimensional nine-year-old version of him is the only one who'll be around tonight. I wonder why it hurts so much that he's not here yet, why that feels like the biggest rejection of all.

I notice Julian strolling through, which reminds me of Elaine and prompts me to ask Jessica where she's gone.

"She went upstairs with Michael," Jessica responds,

and I have to double-check if she really means Michael or if she's got names confused, but apparently he arrived while I was outside, and suddenly it all clicks.

I remember when I liked Tom but I said to Deirdre that I thought he liked her, just because it seemed like the only way to open a dialogue on the subject. Just because I wanted her to say, no, don't be silly, you're the one he likes. So I could have her confirm my hopes without having to suggest it, so we could get onto the topic of who he liked without it seeming as though I was overly confident, convinced I was attractive or interesting enough to be liked by him.

Elaine and Michael. I consider the concept. In a way it makes sense. Maybe. I don't know. It's weird but one of those things that could work out, the way that some couples seem utterly incompatible at the beginning but end up married for the rest of their lives.

They only know each other through me, from evenings hanging out here drinking coffee and watching endless cartoon repeats. But getting to know a prospective significant other through a mutual friend isn't exactly the most unusual thing in the world. And Elaine would be better off with Michael than Julian, and Michael would be better off with her than with Caitriona, and it's actually sort of cool, in a way, these two friends of mine getting together.

Except. Except it's weird. And even though I've

done the very same thing, implied that a guy liked my friend when really I wanted to hear if he liked me, I'm annoyed with Elaine for doing it. I mean, I have a boyfriend, and it's not fair to mess around with my head like that, make me think that Michael might like me.

I can't go upstairs. I don't want to walk in on them doing – whatever it is they might be doing. I wonder how they got past Mum and Jim, but I guess they trust Michael to behave himself and not do anything inappropriate.

Unlike two of Eddie's friends, who, I'm noticing, have smuggled in water bottles filled up with vodka, the way Bonnie and I used to do on the rare occasions when we went to discos.

It's funny, but even after almost a year of going out with Eddie, and knowing his friends, and hanging around with them, I still don't feel like I can go over to them and tell them to be careful. And in between gossiping about school people with Carrie and half-listening to Niamh going on about how her shoes are really hurting her feet but they're so pretty that she can't bear to take them off, I get annoyed with myself about this.

I used to be different. I wasn't always like this. I don't know what happened. Nothing big, nothing drastic, just a series of small changes that I didn't pay any attention to while they were happening but now seem so important, like continuing to put up with Mandy's self-absorption or Dawn's thoughtlessness, like turning into the kind of nice, quiet, calm girl that doesn't let anything bother her even when she should be bothered.

Mum brings out a cake and everyone clusters around. The smokers come back inside, the people having deep meaningful conversations out in the hall return, Michael and Elaine walk in together.

"Happy birthday to you . . ." Mum starts off, and everyone joins in. Bonnie and Deirdre, mature women of the world that they are, sing the "You look like a monkey, and you smell like one too!" version into my left ear.

I hate that everyone's looking at me, so I blow out the candles as quickly as I can, without making a wish, and everyone cheers and Eddie kisses me and it feels so awkward and uncomfortable and it's not about Mum and Jim watching or anything like that, so much as it is about feeling very weird that I'm marking my birthday with a kiss from him.

Because when you kiss someone you have to close your eyes, obviously, and when I open mine again Michael and Elaine have disappeared, and I care much more about that than I do about Eddie's arms around me.

13

Actress

Ok. So maybe I like him. Just a little. Just a teeny tiny bit.

Maybe I like a boy who is not my boyfriend and who is probably right at this moment kissing one of my very good friends and maybe I'm not entitled to be jealous because I have a boyfriend who buys me roses, I have an Eddie, but oh, I am.

I'm jealous. I am so jealous it has an actual physical presence, a huge lump of jealousy somewhere in my chest.

Eddie has his arms around me and I am smiling and chatting to people and being the birthday girl. And it's funny, in primary school I never got to have important parts in the school plays (especially not after that fainting incident) but really, my teachers must have been crazy not to cast me because I'm putting on a magnificent show now, pretending to be happy.

I wonder where they are, what room they're in. I wonder if Michael has been talking to Dan about it, if Dan said, sure, you can have my room, something like that. God, Elaine's probably the only reason he bothered coming. That's all boys that age care about. Putting girls they can potentially kiss ahead of everything else. No wonder he hasn't been expressing irritation with Dan's obsession with Saoirse. He's in exactly the same situation, completely infatuated with Elaine.

I wonder if they're in my room. They'd better not be in my room.

Niamh comes over and repeats the saga of the shoes that hurt too much to wear and cost more than any sane person should spend on footwear.

"But they're just so pretty, aren't they?" she says, lifting up her right foot so I can appreciate them once more.

I nod and smile, even though they're far too sequinned for my taste.

"Here's your cake!" Mum announces, handing me the first slice.

"Looks good," Eddie nods.

I'm not hungry, even though it's chocolate and does

look absolutely gorgeous. "I'm just going to check on something," I tell Eddie.

"Want me to come with you?" he asks.

"Nah, it's ok. Go hang out with the lads." I lean close enough so that Mum doesn't hear before I add, "And make sure they don't get hammered, ok? I'll never be allowed leave the house again if Mum or Jim finds out they've been drinking."

"Ah, Kim, don't worry about it, they'll be fine."

Of course. Of course he doesn't want to go over to his mates and be the one who lectures them about drinking. He doesn't want to be that guy. Great with the romantic gestures, not so great with these minor details, that's Eddie.

"Please," I say, and for a moment I contemplate picking a fight with him over this, but I walk away instead. It wouldn't be about that and I know that. What kind of horrible person am I turning into, to even consider doing something like that? Have a convenient fight with my boyfriend just so I could be legitimately attracted to someone else. It's the kind of thing Dawn would do.

They're coming down the stairs just as I'm about to walk up. Not holding hands. Not looking particularly intimate, as far as I can tell.

"There you are!" Elaine says cheerfully. "We were just coming to get you."

"Here I am!" Suddenly it's a little easier to seem happy.

Michael hands over a silver paper bag with fancy handles, the kind that people give presents in.

Presents!

"Here you go," he says.

"We've just been putting the finishing touches on it," Elaine explains.

"We made some of the things. Because we're cheap," Michael adds.

"Thoughtful. I prefer thoughtful."

"Cheap."

"Thank you so much, guys," I say, pawing through the bag. The card is Elaine's artwork, the cover featuring a cartoon version of me surrounded by presents and balloons. There's a photo collage featuring photos in which I actually look half-decent, and several mix CDs. Looking through them I can tell Michael's picked most of the music, though the one entitled *'Good music from female artists Michael has dismissed because he is a complete music snob'* is, I'm thinking, probably Elaine's contribution. And then there are little things, like silly wind-up cars and glitter pens and the sort of fun but ridiculous things that I love, and, oh dear lord, they've bought me a gigantic bag of chocolate-flavoured coffee.

"We thought you'd like that," Elaine grins as I jump

up and down in delight.

I feel like a two-year-old. A very lucky, very spoiled two-year-old.

I hug them both tightly, genuinely thrilled. Thoughtful, definitely. Not cheap. Thoughtful. Careful. What presents should be and so rarely are.

I love them both so much right now.

As friends, obviously.

With maybe an extra layer on top of that as far as Michael is concerned.

I make sure to put the bag away before we head back to the party, just because I don't want Eddie commenting on it in any way. I don't want him to see it and judge and think it's silly, or to see it and realise that it's the perfect present and someone other than him gave it to me. To realise that his girlfriend prefers the personal touch over textbook romance.

"Make sure you get some cake," I tell them.

I look around the room. There's Mandy, chatting away, and there's Niamh with her expensive accessorising habits, and there are Eddie's friends, being desperately unsubtle about the fact that their bottles do not contain the kind of crystal-clear water that the labels advertise.

And I suddenly have no idea why these people are here. I mean, obviously I do, it's because I invited them, but – the why of inviting them eludes me.

I check my watch. Just after nine. And there we go, I'm back to wishing this party was over, that it was all finished with and we could get on with our lives.

Bad way to think. I need to enjoy the rest of the night. I need to have a good birthday night.

I get talking to Carrie again, going on about this hopeless teacher we have who forgets what language she's supposed to be teaching us – we have her for Italian this year, one of those Transition Year module things, but she keeps speaking to us in Spanish, which is what she teaches the younger students (except according to them, they're getting Italian lessons from her instead).

Deirdre and Bonnie join us for a discussion on the merits of several of Eddie's friends, resulting in Bonnie approaching Vodka Drinker Number One and asking for his number.

"That's not water they're drinking, you know," she tells me upon her return.

I nod. "I know. I said it to Eddie but he doesn't want to go over and be a spoilsport."

"Oooooh!" Deirdre and Bonnie say in unison.

"What?"

"Trouble in paradise," Deirdre says.

I didn't realise I sounded annoyed with Eddie. That I'd slipped up. "No, it's fine. I know how he feels. It's not a big deal."

"Are you sure?" Bonnie asks.

I grin. "Yeah. It's all going to be ok. Don't worry." Because worrying is pointless, and because it doesn't stop the inevitable, anyway.

"Well, if you like her so much, what the hell are you doing with me?" someone screeches from the hallway.

We can hear it even over the music and everyone else in the room talking. Even before I realise who it is, I recognise the familiarity of this situation.

Mandy and her public break-ups. Here we go again.

Everyone pauses for a moment to hear the response, but it's incoherent, given in that teenage-guy-mumble that's almost impossible to understand.

"You *obviously* like her, stop pretending you don't!"

Mumble mumble mumble.

"You've been staring at her all night! And you've only been kissing me when you know she's looking. It's so obvious that you just want to make her jealous."

Silence.

I look for Elaine. She's staring determinedly at the floor. I edge my way over to her. Jessica follows a moment later.

"This clearly isn't working out," Mandy announces, which the entire house has already realised.

"You ok?" I ask Elaine.

She continues her staring match with the ground.

"Was he really looking at me all night?"

"I don't know," I say honestly.

"He was definitely looking at you some of the time," Jessica offers.

"We already know that he wants to make you jealous," I remind her.

"He's so – " She doesn't finish her sentence, just shrugs. "I'm going to go talk to him."

She leaves the room at the same time as Mandy comes back in. Everyone tries to pretend that they weren't listening in to that heart-warming discussion she and Julian were having.

Mum and Jim are exchanging amused looks with each other, as though to comment on how *dramatic* teenagers are these days. This from the people who think that alcohol addiction will seize me if a single drop of wine passes my lips and that my going upstairs with a boy is enough to result in a whole set of grandchildren for them.

"I'm going to head, Kim," Mandy tells me, gathering up her bag and coat. She looks like she's about to cry, so I hug her even though I'm still a bit annoyed about her relating that story earlier. The break-up trauma seems to cancel it out a little.

I walk her to the door, noticing that Julian and Elaine are sitting in the study together and hoping Mandy doesn't see them.

"We should hang out sometime," Mandy says as she steps outside, adhering to the social niceties even right after she's just broken up with her boyfriend. "I'll give you a ring soon."

I nod and smile and know that it isn't true. Mandy doesn't keep in touch with people. Other people have to make the effort.

As I close the door it occurs to me that I don't need to keep making that effort unless I want to.

And when I check my watch again it's almost eleven and people are starting to drift away, starting to think about getting home.

It's almost over. Nearly there. The event which has caused me infinitely more worry and concern than it was worth is almost over.

A very significant part of me is hoping that once the party's over and everything goes back to normal, everything will be ok with me and Eddie too. I'll appreciate the roses and I'll appreciate how lucky I am and I will want him to kiss me and hold me and be my boyfriend.

I'm trying very hard not to listen to the part of me that tells me that things can't ever go back to normal. Very very hard.

"We should hang out sometime," Mandy says, as we stand outside, adhering to the social niceties even though she's just ended up with her boyfriend. "I'll give you a ring soon."

I nod and smile and know that it isn't true. Mandy doesn't keep in touch with people. Other people have to make the effort.

As I close the door it occurs to me that I don't need to keep making the effort just because I want to.

And when I check my watch again it's almost eleven and people are starting to drift away, starting to think about getting home.

It's almost over. Nearly there. The event which has caused me immeasurably more worry and concern than it was probably worth is almost over.

[illegible] part of me is [illegible] and everything will be [illegible] with me and [illegible] I'll appreciate the [illegible] and I'll appreciate [illegible] and I'll want him to [illegible] and hold me and be my boyfriend.

[illegible]

[illegible] I'll deal with this.

[illegible]

14

Birthday Girl

"Kim." That's Jim, sounding not too thrilled with me. "One of the young lads is outside getting sick everywhere. Do you know anything about this?"

"Who is it?" I follow him outside to where this guy – yes, yes it's Vodka Drinker Number Two – is throwing up in the grass.

I approach him. "You ok?"

He nods once, face pale, before depositing what's left of his dinner, it looks like, onto the ground. Lovely.

"Have you been drinking?" Jim demands.

I roll my eyes in a Pearl-esque fashion before turning around to face him and going, "I'll deal with this."

"You most certainly will not. How old are you,

sonny? Do your parents know you drink? Do you know how stupid it is to be doing that at your age?"

And as much as I can see Jim's point about how it's a bit idiotic to be in the kind of state where you're puking in someone's garden at what is supposed to be a civilised gathering, I wish he'd shut up.

"Jim, leave it," I say, but he's already launched into a lecture about the foolishness of underage drinking and the dangers of alcohol poisoning, despite the fact that from the looks of it there's no alcohol – or anything else, for that matter – actually left in Vodka Drinker's system to poison him.

I run back into the house and drag Eddie outside.

"Oh, shit," Eddie says.

I just nod.

"I'll make sure he gets home ok." He kisses me. "Talk to you tomorrow."

"See you," I say as he steps in to rescue his friend from the wrath of Jim. They leave via the side-gate, and I can hear another round of vomiting happen before they make it out onto the road. Fantastic.

Jim is not happy. "That's disgusting, Kim."

"I know. He's an idiot."

"I've a good mind to call his parents and let them know what their son's been up to," he continues. "It's not on, drinking at his age. Honestly. Stupid boy."

"Mmm-hmmm."

"Do you have his number? I could call them now."

"I don't, sorry."

"What's his last name?"

"Jim. Leave it. Really. Eddie will talk to him. It's better if it comes from a friend instead of the parents, you know that."

And it actually works. Jim nods thoughtfully and agrees with me. I decide not to mention that the kind of talking Eddie will be doing will not be "Oh, don't drink, it's bad for you" but more "For God's sake, what kind of lightweight are you?"

Back inside, Jim goes to relate the story to Mum – in the kitchen, thankfully, away from my friends – and I inform Vodka Drinker Number One that his mate has gone home, which frees him up to go chat with Bonnie again. The crowd's thinned out considerably now; once the primary-school crowd head off there's only a few people left. Susan and her boyfriend, Carrie, Jessica and Michael. They've managed to all fit onto the one couch, the one which is only designed for three people.

"Any room for me?" I ask, and find myself sitting on Michael's lap.

Well, not so much find myself sitting there as head directly for it. But only because I'd be too heavy for Carrie or Jessica. I'd crush them.

Yes. That's my excuse.

It's not like it's the first time I've ever sat on his lap. This couch gets plenty of action – we know from experience you can fit at least ten people on it, though not particularly comfortably. So I have sat on his lap before. Several times.

I've just never sat there while being as aware of him as I am now.

"Elaine and Julian still in the study?" I ask the couch at large.

"Apparently," Jessica says.

I can feel him breathe.

"What exactly is the story there?" Carrie wants to know.

"She's the ex, isn't she?" Susan says.

"Yeah," Jessica and I chime. I let her explain. "They were going out for ages, madly in love and all that, broke up a couple of months ago – they'd been fighting for a while, we kinda knew before they did that it was going to end sooner or later. So he turns up with that girl Mandy, but they've only been going out for a few weeks, and he apparently spends the whole night trying to make Elaine jealous."

"They ran into each other a few days ago and he went on about how great his new girlfriend was," I add. "But Mandy – well, she's had a lot of boyfriends."

"Very tactful there, Kim," Susan grins.

"Speaking of which, where's yours?" Carrie asks.

"Boyfriend," she clarifies when I look puzzled.

"Oh, right," I say, at which everyone laughs and various ditzy blonde references are made. "He's gonc. One of his friends got sick so he's looking after him."

"Knight in shining armour," Jessica smiles.

"Yeah, all he needs is a white horse and he's set," I say.

Bonnie and her new boy-toy join us, now holding hands. I pretend not to notice, but when she catches my eye I grin at her.

"We're going to head off," she says, which means I have to leave the couch and the lap in order to do the hugging thing and to thank her for coming and for the present and all that. They leave together, and somehow I suspect they're going to make that walk home a very long one.

"We should really get going too," Susan says, and then there's a flurry of activity because suddenly everyone's a sheep and getting ready to leave.

Everyone except Michael. I hug and I thank and I watch people walk away and then I return to the couch and he's still there.

He grins. "I have no sense of etiquette."

I laugh. "I can see that." I sit down next to him this time.

"I'll go if you want."

"Nah, it's all right. Did you have a good night?"

He nods. "Yeah."

"How was the music? Did it meet your exacting standards?"

"It was acceptable. You should listen to those CDs, though. Some great stuff on them."

"I will." I pause. "Thank you so much for that."

He shrugs.

"You know," I begin, and oh I can't believe I'm doing this because it's a step I can't take back, but I am, it seems, "when you and Elaine were off together, I actually thought that, you know, you two –"

He raises an eyebrow. "Really?"

"Yeah."

"We're not."

"I know."

"You and your one-track mind."

"Yeah, I know."

"How about you? Good night?"

"It was – interesting," I say.

"You got roses," he says.

"I did. That was weird."

"They're not really your thing, are they?"

"No. No, they're not." I sigh and sink back into the couch.

He looks at me for a moment and I think something's going to happen, but it doesn't. I'm nervous, jittery, anticipatory, but then he gets up and says, "We should check in on those two."

Oh. Right. Elaine and Julian. Yes, we should. I suppose.

We're out in the hall, and he puts his ear to the door instead of just knocking.

Can you hear anything? I mouth.

He shakes his head and shrugs.

"Just leave them," I whisper.

But we don't. We stay listening in at the door trying to hear what's going on, because we are curious. Well, nosy and gossipy. Same thing.

Julian is mumbling.

"I wish he'd enunciate," I whisper in Michael's ear.

"Doesn't he know we want to know what's going on?" he replies.

I'm still concentrating on trying to get something out of the mumbling when Michael checks his watch. "Hey. It's after midnight."

"Really? I didn't know it was that late."

What it means doesn't hit me until he says, "Happy birthday, Kimmie."

And there's something about the way he says it, or the way he looks, or the way we're so close right now – there's *something*, anyway, and it makes me lean over and press my lips against his.

My heart is pounding and my legs are a little shaky and my mouth is on his and we're kissing. Not a friend kind of kiss, not a peck on the lips, but a proper dizzying kiss that's about wanting and needing and finally having. He tastes of coffee and chocolate and he kisses *exceptionally* well and what on earth have I been playing at all these years not to have been doing this?

I want, I want. Right now I want all the things from him that I have never quite been sure about before, all those things that involve real intimacy and taking clothes off. I want him. He's right here and even that isn't close enough and –

Yes, that would be a key turning in the lock.

Dan opens the front door just as we separate. I have no idea what he saw, if he can tell.

"Hey. Good night?" he asks.

All I can do is nod.

"You?" Michael asks him.

Dan grins. "Yeah."

Michael laughs as he gets his coat. "Night," he says, directing it at both of us. And he's gone.

I stare after him, not sure if he left because Dan got here or because of me. Because of – did I really just kiss him? Did that just happen?

"Ok," Dan says, looking at Michael go. "What. The. Hell."

"Hmmm?" I say, as though I have no idea what he's talking about.

"You and Mike. You and Mike. Dude."

"What are you, a surfer? Who on earth says 'dude'? Honestly." I take a deep breath. "So you and Saoirse had fun tonight, huh?"

"Uh-huh."

"Good. Thrilled for you. I'm going to go to bed now."

"Ok. Everyone gone?"

"Yeah – no. Crap." I'm halfway up the stairs before I remember that everyone is not gone. Back down to tap on the door of the study.

"Elaine? Everything ok in there?" I call.

She emerges a moment later, followed by Julian.

"Hey. Sorry, Kim, I didn't realise how late it was. Is everyone else gone already?"

I nod. "Yeah. It's fine, don't worry about it." I look at her and try to figure out what exactly's happened between the two of them. It's not like I can ask with him there.

"I'll talk to you tomorrow, ok?" she says as she gets her coat.

"Ok," I nod. I watch them leave. They're not holding hands but they're walking close enough to one another to be touching.

I try to analyse their situation but every time I think about what might have happened in that room, what they might have said to one another, I keep thinking of Michael and what happened outside of that room.

I kissed Michael.
I have an Eddie.
And I kissed Michael.
And Dan knows.
"You and Mike," he says again.
"I know," I say. "Dude."

15

Couch Potato

Sunday is supposed to be a day of rest, right? So I spend my Sunday resting. Actually, I spend it sitting on the couch, eyes glued to the television. It's about the only thing I feel capable of doing.

"You look tired," Mum notes.

"Mmmm," I say. That's what happens when you don't get much sleep the night before because you've kissed someone who is not your boyfriend. Tiredness ensues.

Dan comes in at one stage. "Hey, your phone was just ringing."

"I'll look at it later," I say, even though I have no intention of doing such a thing. My phone is up in my bedroom and I'm downstairs, avoiding it. Avoiding people. People are too much today. The people on television will have to suffice.

The people on television often kiss people who they're not supposed to. There is a lot of that happening on Sunday afternoon repeats.

Analysing this – in a vague, tired sort of way – is about the only way I can think about last night without really thinking about it.

I conclude that there are various reasons why people kiss people who they are not in relationships with. For reasons other than the fact that watching stable and steady relationships progress does not make for interesting television, I mean.

For starters, sometimes people are kissed rather than being the ones who initiate the kiss, in which case their level of guilt is alleviated. If they are kissed and push the other person away, then they have no reason to feel guilty. If they kiss back, then that's a problem. But it's not as bad as being the one who kisses.

Because if you're the one who kisses, if you're the one who takes that first step and makes a move on someone else when you're in a relationship, then – well, then you're in trouble. And your relationship is.

Sometimes it happens because there's something missing in your relationship. You're hurt or you're lonely, so you go for someone else, anyone else, just to make yourself feel better. It isn't about the other person so much as it is about you and what you're not getting from the person you're with.

Sometimes it's just about being attracted to someone else. About finding a specific someone else who's right for you. But if that's the case then the whole thing about something missing in your relationship still applies, doesn't it? I mean, if you're into someone else, if you want to act on an attraction instead of just recognising that someone else is cute, then that says something about your relationship, right?

I used to think it did. It used to be black and white. If you like someone else then you shouldn't be in a relationship. End of story.

But then there's Dawn and people like her, people who can actually like someone else while still adoring the people they're with. Not that I want to be like Dawn. But it's happened to Bonnie, too. She's liked other people even when in relationships. And sure, I've always told her that the liking was clearly a sign that there was something not-quite-right in her relationship, but maybe I just didn't know what I was talking about.

I wasn't in a relationship with Tom long enough to be attracted to anyone else, and anyway, Tom was the sort of guy who demanded your attention one hundred percent of the time. Plenty of melodrama and angst there. And then before him there wasn't anyone particularly special. There were a handful of drunken kisses in parks, people Bonnie and I sort-of knew but never talked to when sober, but that was it. No one who was a boyfriend or anything more than an acquaintance, really. How can I be sure that it isn't just normal to have a wandering eye after eleven and a half months with the same person?

It's just that everyone else who seems to be into other people – well, they get restless after a much shorter period of time. Dawn after maybe five weeks, Bonnie after two months or so. When Elaine broke up with Julian it took her a while to actually do the deed because she wasn't sure whether it was the standard six-month-restlessness thing that seems to happen or if there were genuine problems there.

I really thought Eddie and I were different.

On the television, there is a bitter guy talking about how his wife cheated on him with his best friend. You're supposed to feel sorry for him. You know because that kind of music is playing in the background. You're supposed to hate the wife for what she's done to him.

At least Eddie and I aren't married. At least Michael isn't his best friend. At least it was just a kiss. Even if it was a kiss that was interrupted by something external instead of a conscious decision. It's still not really an ideal situation.

I am a cheater. I'm Laura, Take Two as far as Eddie is concerned. I can't believe I'm a *cheater.*

Dan comes in again, slumps down in the armchair next to me.

"What happened with you and Eddie?" he asks.

I shrug. "Nothing happened."

He sits up straight. "You're still with him?"

I glare at him. "Yes."

"Oh. Shit."

"Yes," I reply to Dan's gift for stating the obvious.

"What are you going to do?"

I sigh. "Watch TV. Not think about it." Which is proving to be difficult. How do you *not* think about something like this?

"He's a nice guy," Dan says.

"I know, I know," I snap. "And I'm a horrible person for kissing someone else. I *know.*"

"No, Michael."

"Oh," I say, and am quiet for a bit. I want to ask Dan what he knows. Whether Michael likes me or not. But I don't know if Michael would even share that information with Dan – I mean, isn't there some boy thing about not going after each other's sisters? And even if they do, they wouldn't talk to the brother about liking them, would they?

And besides, I'm beginning to understand why Dan

doesn't talk to me much about girls. There are some things you just can't discuss comfortably with your siblings. For him the line is in-depth analysis of his relationship with any girl, and for me – for me it's this. I can't talk to him about Michael.

Michael's his best friend. They have an entire world that doesn't include me. One time, when they were in third year, the two of them got suspended from school and I still have no idea what happened. Maybe it was something stupid like getting caught smoking, even though neither of them smoke now; maybe it was for mitching or for playing a prank or for fighting. I don't know. They won't tell me. It's just another one of those secrets they have, like where they hid their 'treasure' when we were kids. They won't tell me that, either.

So I suppose the only way to find out whether Michael likes me or not, whether he kissed me back just because I was kissing him or whether he kissed me back because he wanted to, is to actually ask him.

Or is that even important? Shouldn't I be putting Eddie first right now? What am I going to tell him? Do I need to tell him?

Dan takes the remote control and switches over to cartoons.

"Hey!" I object.

"You're not watching this, you're staring into space," he says.

Dan and I battle it out over the remote control all the time but today I think he has a point. Besides, people cheat on their significant others slightly less in cartoons, which means the television is now working much more effectively as a means of distracting myself from this messy, messy situation.

16

Schoolgirl

It seems incredible that no one in school can tell what happened. Or even that *something's* happened. I feel like it's written all over my face. I cheated on my boyfriend. I am the kind of girl who cheats on her boyfriend. I am no longer nice Kim, but evil Kim. And everyone else is just talking about work experience or the concert or last night's television shows, and they have no idea what's going on with me.

"So Jason goes to get us drinks and this random guy comes up to me and starts talking to me, and oh my God, you should've seen him, he was so gorgeous. So I was like, I'm here with my boyfriend, and he's like, oh, how's that going for you . . ."

I tune out a little bit during Dawn's description of

her encounter with yet another guy during the concert, and when I tune back in she's at the part where she has his number even though she's not going to text him unless, of course, something were to happen with her and Jason.

I wonder if kissing Michael is the sort of thing that Dawn would do. Not kissing Michael specifically – though he might be her type, especially because he's older – but kissing a friend while still in a relationship.

I could ask her for advice, except that I've spent most of the past week thinking of Dawn as exactly the sort of person I *don't* want to be when it comes to matters of the heart. And I don't want to tell her about this, anyway. It's my secret, for the moment.

I look around and realise that I don't want to talk to any of these people about it, except maybe Bonnie. Deirdre, who has no objections to rolling her eyes over Dawn's romantic dramas when we're alone, is listening intently to what she has to say, and Orla's busy texting someone because she is that sort of person who communicates almost entirely via text messages, and these other girls are – nice, but they're not my people.

They don't know me well enough to come up with mix CDs that suit me perfectly, like the *'Songs by great bands that you, Kim, have foolishly ignored up until now because of their silly names'* CD that I put on repeat last night (quite possibly because I'm slightly infatuated with that nice young gentleman who put it together, but the music is actually really good). They're not the people I spend most of my out-of-school time with. They're not Michael or Elaine or Dan or Eddie (oh, don't think about Eddie right now). They're just girls that I ended up hanging around with because – I don't know. I guess because Bonnie was friendly with some of them and I was good friends with her and somehow a group began to form.

I think about the Gaeltacht crowd, the friends I made on my own terms. I wonder how many of them would fit into my normal life, like Elaine, if they lived nearby. And I know that summer-friends aren't always the same once you get back to school and all that, but right now I really want one of those late-night get-togethers in the woods. I'm craving that level of intensity in my friendships, and Dawn and the others just can't provide it.

And, of course, if I was back in the Gaeltacht I'd be miles and miles away from these problematic boys. It'd help.

After break, instead of our usual session on current affairs, all of our year gets a talk from the guidance counsellor about how we can Most Effectively Utilise Our Experiences from last week and Make Informed Decisions About Our Futures.

"Sometimes it can be even more useful to find out what you *don't* want to do," she says earnestly, "so don't worry if all you learned last week was that you definitely don't want to be a lawyer or an engineer or a teacher. It's all relevant."

I doodle on the cover of an A4 pad and consider whether I learned anything last week or not. I wonder whether I would be able to deal with someone like Pearl for an entire year if I was her teacher. Maybe if I was older I'd be able to, or maybe that's what they teach you when you go and do a degree in education. Maybe if I was an actual teacher there wouldn't be a problem in the first place because I'd have that title, that automatic respect thing working in my favour. It's only in secondary school that kids start really questioning authority, I think.

Maybe I'm just not cut out for dealing with kids in an academic environment. Maybe I need to be the cool baby-sitter who gets them playing games instead of the mean teacher making them do their work.

"Think about yourself in ten years," the guidance counsellor is saying. "Can you see yourself working in that particular job every single day? Does it fit with any other goals you might have set for yourself?"

I think what she actually means is whether we plan on having kids at that point. I imagine myself at twenty-six. Oh, wow, that's old! I mean, not *old* old, not like Mum and Dad and Jim and Annelise, but it's the kind of age where you have an actual career and a mortgage and are married and have kids and all that. You've achieved things, or are supposed to have, anyway. You're a real grown-up, not a technical one, but a real one, the kind that everyone recognises as such.

I imagine coming home from a day of teaching little kids. Maybe I'm stressed because Pearl has reproduced and her spawn are just as irritating as she is. So I get in the door, and my husband is there to make me a cup of tea and massage my shoulders. Because he'll be decent enough to do these things, that's why we got married.

My imaginary future husband is wearing Michael's face.

What, I want to marry the guy now? This is ridiculous. I am not the kind of girl who imagines an entire future with someone just because we've kissed once.

I'm only thinking in the long-term now because we're sitting here being told to, I reassure myself. And Michael's only there because I've been thinking about him, and of course I've been thinking about him, because there was kissing and I have a boyfriend and it's generally all very very bad.

What do I want? What do I not want? I have no idea.

When the guidance counsellor hands out forms she's done up which we are supposed to fill out for our own benefit, I write that my experiences last week have encouraged me to keep an open mind about teaching. Because it'd be silly to dismiss something you've considered and wanted for a while now just because of one experience.

It would, right?

17

Agony Aunt

In sharp contrast to Sunday's avoidance tactics, I check my phone obsessively on Monday evening, but there's nothing important there. Nothing from Michael, and I don't know whether I'm relieved or disappointed. I've never been afraid to send a simple text message before but now even the thought makes me unbelievably nervous. Especially because he hasn't sent me anything. I have text messages from various people wishing me a happy birthday and thanking me for the party, but nothing from him.

I wonder if he'll come over this evening. I wonder if he and Dan talked about it in school today. I would consider rethinking my policy on avoiding Michael-related discussion with Dan, but he's not even here.

Off with Saoirse again. On a Monday evening. It must be love. Either that or he's found himself a more fun method of procrastinating than ranting about the injustice of our educational system.

I put on *'The greatest songs of all time, if time were the 1990s, which admittedly wasn't the best era for music but just give these a try, ok?'* (one of the CDs I haven't listened to yet) and turn on the computer. I have seven new emails, and every single one of them is spam.

When my phone beeps, I practically throw myself across the room to where it's attached to the charger, and pick it up. Message from Eddie about whether I'm busy on Wednesday.

I'm not. And within a few minutes we have plans to go to the cinema on Wednesday evening, which at the very least will mean that I won't have to talk to him for two hours, which means I won't have to lie to him.

* * *

Pretentious Artsy Chick says: **Hey, you!**

Kimperfection says: **Hi! What's going on?**

Pretentious Artsy Chick says: **Will tell you in a sec. Sorry I didn't call yesterday, I was kind of avoiding people all day.**

* * *

Ah, yes. I know that feeling.

Most of the girls from school would never say that. You're not supposed to ever avoid people or not be in the mood for chatting.

I'm starting to think Elaine's way is the way to go.

* * *

Kimperfection says: **No problem. Everything ok? What happened with Julian??**

Pretentious Artsy Chick says: **Think we might be getting back together. MAYBE.**

Kimperfection says: **Seriously?**

Pretentious Artsy Chick says: **Yeah. Not sure though.**

Kimperfection says: **So things are definitely over with him and Mandy, then?**

Pretentious Artsy Chick says: **Looks like it. He's not going back to her even if she wants it, so . . . yeah. They're over.**

Pretentious Artsy Chick says: **And he said it was over between them even if something didn't happen with us, so . . . that's good, right? I'm not under any pressure.**

Kimperfection says: **Yeah, that is good. You can avoid being the shameless hussy who breaks people up!**

Pretentious Artsy Chick says: **I know! Yay! Even though I think people are still going to think that. I mean, Mandy completely blamed the whole thing on me. Very publicly.**

Kimperfection says: **Yeah, but anyone who knows Mandy and her crazy break-up patterns will know not to take her too seriously. It's not your fault anyway – you can't control his behaviour. I mean, come on, your powers of seduction aren't THAT great.**

Pretentious Artsy Chick says: **Haha. Thanks.**

Kimperfection says: **So do you think it's going to work out this time?**

* * *

Oh, that sounds judgemental, like I'm telling her she's foolish to believe that a second chance with Julian could produce anything worth having. I quickly type some more.

* * *

Kimperfection says: **I mean, are you going to go for**

it? 'Cause obviously there's still something there . . .

Pretentious Artsy Chick says: **Yeah. There is. When I was talking to him at your party it was just like it used to be. I mean, we get along so well, we've a lot in common, and I miss him, you know? I miss having him around.**

* * *

The old Kim would have reminded her, nicely but firmly, that just because you miss someone doesn't mean that you should get back together with him. She might have also reminded Elaine that the conflict that led to the break-up probably hasn't just disappeared, and added that a guy who has just been dumped by his girlfriend isn't in the best position to make decisions about relationships right about now.

The new Kim has a different perspective on life. She's not sure what it is yet, but she knows that she doesn't think romantic entanglements are quite as clear-cut as she once did.

Also, she appears to really enjoy thinking about herself in the third person.

* * *

Kimperfection says: **I hope it works out for you.**

Pretentious Artsy Chick says: **Thanks, hon. Me too.**

Pretentious Artsy Chick says: **So what's going on with you? Were the parentals satisfied with the behaviour at the party?**

Kimperfection says: **They were ok. You know the guys who were drinking? Eddie's mates?**

Pretentious Artsy Chick says: **Oh, yeah. Did Jim catch them?**

Kimperfection says: **Caught one of them, 'cause he was sick outside. Not happy about it at ALL, but he gave your man a lecture on the spot and he's only brought it up once since.**

* * *

Which for Jim is really something of a record. I think he's a bit disappointed, actually. He imagined having to stave off a drunken teenage orgy, and all he got was one idiotic boy to give out to.

He and Mum might actually have to start trusting me now.

* * *

Pretentious Artsy Chick says: **Uh-oh, not good! Nothing was said about people going off together into small rooms for hours at a time, then?**

Kimperfection says: **No, you and Julian are safe from the wrath of Jim, don't worry.**

Pretentious Artsy Chick says: **Cool.**

Kimperfection says: **Hey, I've been listening to those CDs from you and Michael. They're amazing.**

* * *

It's a not-very-subtle way to bring the conversation around to Michael, but oh well.

* * *

Pretentious Artsy Chick says: **Yay! Glad you like them. He spent aaaaages on them, you know.**

Kimperfection says: **Really?**

Pretentious Artsy Chick says: **Yeah.**

Kimperfection says: **Well, he's a music junkie.**

Pretentious Artsy Chick says: **Sure, yeah, that's all it is . . .**

Kimperfection says: **Care to elaborate on that?**

Pretentious Artsy Chick says: **Come on, you know he likes you. I mean, I sort of suspected, before, but then we started putting together your present and I saw how he was about it and it was just so OBVIOUS.**

* * *

And there it is, on the screen in front of me. Confirmation of that initial throwaway statement that has had me thinking all kinds of things over the last few weeks. Michael likes me. Sure, it's only an opinion, but it's an informed one, and Elaine is good with these kinds of things.

He likes me.

* * *

Kimperfection says: **Yeah, but he hasn't said anything to me.**

Pretentious Artsy Chick says: **Would you tell someone in a year-long relationship that you liked them?**

Kimperfection says: **Maybe. If I really liked them.**

Pretentious Artsy Chick says: **Really?**

Kimperfection says: **Ok. Maybe not. But still. He could say something. He should say something.**

Pretentious Artsy Chick says: **What, so you can have your ego stroked?**

Kimperfection says: **Exactly! No, just . . .**

Pretentious Artsy Chick says: **You want to break his heart into little itty-bitty pieces?**

Kimperfection says: **NO!**

Pretentious Artsy Chick says: **Oh my God. You like him.**

* * *

If I admit it to Elaine it's out there in the universe. It's confirmation that I am the kind of girl who gets crushes even though she has a boyfriend. Do I want her to know this?

* * *

Kimperfection says: **Nah, I just – I think it'd just be easier for him if he said something.**

Pretentious Artsy Chick says: **Maybe. I don't know. I don't get boys.**

Kimperfection says: **Yeah, me neither. Oooh, have to go – dinner's on the table. Talk to you later!**

* * *

Dinner is not on the table. Dinner tonight is all over the place, because Mum and Jim are working late and Dan has his thing with Saoirse. Dinner is me in front of the television with a pizza and a glass of milk, wondering when exactly I started lying to my friends.

And then I realise, suddenly, that I started lying to

my friends when I was ten years old, when I realised that you couldn't show how you were really feeling because people got angry with you or they laughed at you for doing stupid things. When I was twelve and I started secondary school and I went along with the trends in fashion that Dawn and Bonnie followed, even though some of the outfits were ridiculous and uncomfortable. When I was thirteen and pretended to like all the same music that Dan and Michael did, even though some of it was horrible.

When I was fifteen and invited people I didn't especially like or have much in common with anymore to my birthday party. When I was fifteen and didn't tell Mandy that I was annoyed with her, didn't tell Dawn her attitude bothered me, didn't tell Dan that I really wanted him there for my party.

When I was sixteen and I told my boyfriend that I'd see him on Wednesday without mentioning the fact that I had kissed someone else after he left the party. When I told one of my best friends that I didn't like the guy that I haven't been able to stop thinking about.

I'll tell her. The next time I'm talking to her, I'll tell her. I'll tell Eddie I kissed him. I'll tell Michael – I don't know what I'll tell him. Not yet.

But I do know that he likes me, apparently, and that's enough to give me the courage to send him a text message.

*   *   *

Hey. Think we need to talk. You around any time this week?

*   *   *

When I flip through the channels, there's a woman kicking her husband out of the house after having cheated on her.

I try not to think about what an Eddie scorned will look like.

Hey. Think we need to talk. You around any time this week?

8

When I flip through the channels, there's a woman [illegible] her husband [illegible]. Bored after having cheated on him.

I try not to think about what an adultery would look like.

It's Wednesday and he hasn't replied. Since it hasn't even been a whole twenty-four hours yet – but – still. It's Michael. Why hasn't he replied? Why oh why oh why?

"Everything ok with Eddie?" Bonnie asks me during Media Studies (i.e. an excuse for us to watch lots of films and read magazines).

"Yeah. It's fine, why?"

She shrugs. "You keep checking your phone. That usually means there's something going on with a boy."

"You read too much into things," I smile.

"So what's the big emergency then?"

"I'm just waiting for someone to get back to me. That's all."

"Who is this someone?" she wants to know, and

18

Stranger

It's Tuesday and he hasn't replied. Sure, it hasn't even been a whole twenty-four hours yet, but – still. It's Michael. Why hasn't he replied? Why oh why oh why?

"Everything ok with Eddie?" Bonnie asks me during Media Studies (i.e. an excuse for us to watch lots of films and read magazines).

"Yeah, it's fine, why?"

She shrugs. "You keep checking your phone. That usually means there's something going on with a boy."

"You read too much into things," I smile.

"So what's the big emergency then?"

"I'm just waiting for someone to get back to me. That's all."

"Who is this someone?" she wants to know, and

then looks at me closely. "Is this a *male* someone? A someone other than Eddie?"

I laugh as though what she is saying is ridiculous and not entirely and completely accurate. "It's just – you know my friend Michael? I think he might be annoyed with me over something, and – it's weird. We don't ever really fight properly, we always make up really quickly, you know?"

She nods. "Yeah. So how long have you been into him, hmm?"

"What? I'm –" And I can feel my face going red – there's no way I can get out of this.

The bell rings. It's a double class but the teacher pauses the video to give us a break. Bonnie and I stay in our seats.

"Hang on a sec – you were sitting on his lap! On Saturday! You were sitting on his lap!"

I suppose she wasn't as wrapped up in Vodka Drinker Number One as I thought.

"Where was Eddie during this?" she demands. "Oh, no, I remember, he went home early. Did you two have a fight or something?"

"No, everything's the same with Eddie," I say.

"With the fencing. And the roses," she says.

"Yep," I say, and then we both giggle.

"You did seem a bit – I don't know, *off* with him. At the party. Are you thinking about breaking up with him?"

I have to laugh at how quickly she moves from 'a bit off' to 'breaking up'. "No," I say. And then I decide to be honest with her. Because I need to talk to someone, and Bonnie is a good friend, and she's here right now. "But I think he might want to break up with me."

"Why? Has he said anything?"

I shake my head. "Nah. But – ok, look, don't spread this around." Which is really code for "I don't want Dawn's opinion on this so don't tell her, ok?"

"I promise. What?"

"I did something at the party. Something not-very-nice."

I look at her and she knows.

"You scored Michael!"

"That I did," I say.

It's funny. Saying it out loud and talking about it doesn't make it any worse. In fact, it seems to make it less serious. The words can escape into the atmosphere and nothing drastic has happened.

"Does Eddie know?"

"I'm seeing him tomorrow. I'm going to tell him then."

"You could just not tell him," Bonnie suggests.

"I'm going to tell him," I say firmly.

She nods. "Ok. Fair enough."

I reach into the pocket of my school skirt and check my phone again. Bonnie just laughs.

He still hasn't replied.

And he still hasn't replied by the time I get home from school, several hours later. *Is* he annoyed with me? Because I kissed him? Because I didn't get in touch with him right away? Because of something else? Does he share Eddie's views on the kinds of things that are too important to discuss via text, even though I only alluded to the kiss? Does he think the opposite and wonders why I'm avoiding mentioning it directly?

I want to see him. The funny thing about talking about a boy to your friends is that it makes you even more excited about it all, even if you know you shouldn't be. Bonnie knows what happened and now it's out there, floating around. It's something I chose to tell her instead of her stumbling upon it the way Dan did.

And somehow that makes it more about the kiss than the cheating. Michael instead of Eddie. Sure, I still don't think it was the moral and pure thing to do, kissing someone who wasn't my boyfriend, but I don't feel as guilty as I think I should.

Because I really, really wanted to do it. Maybe if it was an honest mistake, a spur-of-the-moment thing with someone like, say, Julian, I'd regret it and feel horrible right now, but it's – it's Michael. It's *Michael.*

I hear a key turning in the lock and head straight for the front door, ready to ask Dan if he knows anything, ready to ignore my comfort levels for the sake of getting information.

There are two boys in school uniform.

"I'll wait outside," Michael mutters to Dan, walking out again.

"What's going on?" I ask Dan, who's busy throwing his bag and school jacket on the floor.

"Nothing," Dan says.

I roll my eyes. "Yeah. Right. Ok." And I go outside, to where Michael is leaning against the wall, staring into space.

"Hi," I say tentatively.

He looks at me as though I'm a complete stranger, and then turns his gaze elsewhere.

"What's going on, Michael?"

He ignores me.

"Can't we just talk for a minute?" I ask him. Can't he just see me, for a moment?

"No, we can't 'talk'," he says slowly and quietly, still not looking me in the eye. "I don't want to talk to you right now."

"Mikey," I say, moving closer to him, because maybe if I can just hug him or something it'll all be ok.

"Don't," he says in that quiet voice again, and then

in a louder, angry voice that I've hardly ever heard him use, "Get away from me!"

Two minutes later I am having the kind of sobbing-in-the-shower experience that I thought I'd left behind last week.

I suppose that answers the question of whether or not he's annoyed with me. Annoyed doesn't even begin to cover it, really. That voice. Michael's never used that voice with me before. The last time I heard him use it was when he was really upset, right after his grandfather's funeral, and Caitriona was pushing him, trying to get him to talk about it – oh.

At least there's a pattern there. Don't push Michael into trying to talk about things he doesn't want to discuss. I should have known that, but I just really wanted to find out what was going on.

Suddenly it seems less likely that I'll be coming home from work in ten years' time to find Michael there ready to provide massages. The more likely scenario seems to involve him not speaking to me for a very long time, if ever.

I can't believe he's angry with me. I can't believe we're not talking. I mean, we don't fight, ever, really. Not like this. There's been irritation and frustration but never serious anger between us. And mostly the irritation is on my part, anyway, and it gets sorted out quickly and then everything's back to being ok because I can't stand things *not* being ok with us. Mum used to tell me and Dan over and over that we shouldn't ever go to bed angry, and even though it was advice that she clearly never took herself, what with that whole divorce thing, it's stayed with me.

I want to work things out, want to talk about them, not have someone be angry with me. Especially not Michael.

When I get out of the shower and settle down to do my homework, I hit the play button on the CD player, as per usual, only I realise that all the songs remind me of Michael. Well, obviously. He picked them all out. I look through my collection and try to find something neutral, but everything reminds me of him. Even the Lucy Marshall CDs – I can hear his voice in my head criticising her. *"Just because she's a girl doesn't mean you have to like her. Come on, put something good on. Have you heard the new Mystic Rockets song?"*

There is nothing in my CD collection that is not in some way tainted by Michael, even if it's only because I know he wouldn't like this one, or would roll his eyes at that one.

Well. There's one CD. It's the CD that has the song from last New Year's on it. So I stick that on.

I try to write an essay dissecting the film we've been watching in Media Studies, but I keep getting distracted.

I really, really liked Eddie when I met him. I mean, I really did. I saw Bonnie a few days later and we spent the entire time talking about him, about how he was so sweet and chivalrous and interesting and fun and gorgeous and generally the eighth wonder of the world. He was all I wanted to talk about, all I could think about. I did exactly what everyone does when they first meet someone they're crazy about – I babbled. I raved. I bored people to tears. And I didn't care, because it was all so wonderful and magical between us.

That kind of feeling can't last forever. I knew that even then. But I also knew that the closeness that came after that, the solid relationship part – it was good. It was worthwhile. It was special in its own way.

And maybe we haven't had the most solid relationship lately, what with me not telling him vital things like being worried to the point of insomnia over the party, or thinking about Michael more than I should. But that's my problem, right? That's something I did because I was distracted and I wasn't ready to talk about it, and just because we're not fighting outright doesn't mean that I should ignore the usual solution. I need to tell him things.

Except if I tell him about Michael I know how he'll react. Who wants to hear about their girlfriend kissing someone else? Who wants to continue having her as their girlfriend?

Eddie and I used to have something great. We could have that again. Maybe I need to be selective with the things that I tell him. I mean, at the end of the day, it was just a kiss. One kiss.

Maybe I just needed to get it out of my system.

It's not like anything can ever happen with me and Michael. It's not like we're ever going to kiss again. I'll be lucky if he even talks to me at some point in the next year.

And I'd be stupid to throw away what I have with Eddie. Really stupid.

I stare at the almost-blank page in front of me and decide that secondary school teachers are crazy to demand coherent writing from people who clearly have more pressing things on their minds. I set the homework aside and hit repeat on the CD player.

10

Heartbreaker

19

Heartbreaker

Wednesday evening is wet and miserable. And windy, too, so that I'm getting drenched even though I'm under the bus shelter. The bus, of course, is late, and I keep looking at my watch even though I know how pointless and ineffective that is.

I'm supposed to meet Eddie at seven. It is now a quarter to seven, and the bus takes twenty minutes to reach the cinema on a good day. I dig my phone out of my bag – the kind of bag that Niamh would probably cringe at, as it's falling apart and didn't cost the world, but I love it – and send him a message telling him I'm going to be late.

By the time the bus decides to make an appearance, it's nearly seven. Eddie rings me just as I find one of the few available seats.

"Hey," I say, "I'm on my way. Just got on the bus. I'll be there in half an hour."

"Ok. It's getting fairly packed in here – do you want me to just get the tickets now?"

"Yeah, all right. I'll see you in a while."

The bus moves along agonisingly slowly. There's a girl in a seat two rows behind me sharing her life story with the entire bus. Why don't people ever realise that other people can hear them when they're on the phone? I half-listen to the saga and am grateful that at least I haven't had a pregnancy scare or been caught by parents in a very embarrassing situation.

When I finally get to the cinema, bearing a remarkable resemblance to a drowned rat, I'm sure, I kiss Eddie extra-hard to make up for being an evil cheater of a girlfriend, and then he takes my hand and we get into the queue for popcorn and drinks.

"What did you get tickets for?" I ask.

It's for *Getting Over You*, a romantic comedy starring various people I know of but have never actually seen in anything.

"Did you want to see this?" I say, surprised.

He shrugs. "Didn't you?"

I'm about to say no but then I say, "It's fine. Looks good." Actually, there's this animated thing they're showing that looks fantastic, and it's supposed to have a brilliant soundtrack, but we have the tickets for this now. It's weird that Eddie would pick it, though. I don't remember ever saying anything about it.

I buy chocolate – one of those giant bags of Maltesers – and Eddie buys popcorn. I'm not really a popcorn person and he's not really a chocolate person, so we've never had that cheesy-romantic thing where your hands meet while reaching for the next bit of popcorn or anything like that. Then again, by the time we went on our first outing to the cinema, hand-holding was already a familiar activity.

There is nothing new and exciting about Eddie holding my hand in the cinema right now. And normally that's not even an issue, because it's familiar and it's comforting and that means more than any initial flutters and thrills that a new guy in your life causes, but now it can't even be that.

It's just a hand entangled with mine and that's it.

The movie opens with a break-up, which makes me a little fidgety. I hope Eddie doesn't notice. I hold my breath and hope the couple on screen aren't fighting because one of them went off with someone else, but it turns out to be all about lack of consideration and such like, fortunately.

The basic plot of the movie is that these two people keep trying to prove to one another that they're over the other, even though it's blatantly obvious that they're not. There are lots of power ballads and significant glances and, sure enough, they end up together. I'm glad when it's over.

"What did you think?" I ask Eddie, wrinkling up my nose.

"It was ok," he shrugs. "How about you?"

"I thought it was rubbish," I say honestly.

He looks surprised. "Yeah. I guess it kind of was."

"You just said it was ok," I point out.

"Yeah, but I thought you liked it. I didn't want to offend you."

I stare at him in surprise. "That's not – why would I be offended by you having a different opinion?"

"I was just trying to be nice," he says, and it almost sounds angry. So I leave it.

"Do you want to get something in here?" I ask him as we pass by a tiny ice-cream café. He nods, and we go inside.

I realise too late that there's not much he really likes on the menu. It's all sweet rather than savoury stuff. But then it occurs to me that he picked the film without really thinking of me, so it evens out somehow.

I watch him peruse the menu and try to reconcile this guy in front of me with the Eddie I met last New Year's Eve. Back then he listened to me, or seemed to, anyway. He knew I was the girl who preferred indie rock over mushy number-one hits, that I was Kim the person instead of a representative of the species *girl*. I wasn't the kind of girl you needed to tread on eggshells around. I could be talked to like an actual person instead of a prospective girlfriend.

And he was shy and sweet and didn't make assumptions about me, and I wonder how much of that changing is my fault, and how much of it is his, and if maybe we'd have changed anyway.

I am not the kind of girl you buy flowers for, or take to a bad romantic comedy. I am not the kind of girl you lie to about trivial things like films so as not to upset her. I am not that girl. And I don't know if it's the way that I've been acting, or the way Eddie thinks he should treat a girlfriend, or a combination of both, that has got us here, but I do know that it's not *me*.

"Did your friend get home ok on Saturday?" I ask.

He nods. "Yeah. God, he's such an idiot, though. I can't believe he got so pissed at your party."

And how do I reconcile the Eddie who tries to be romantic with the one who wouldn't tell his friends to stop drinking but was still disdainful of the one who got sick from it? Or is that just what sixteen-year-old boys are like – clumsily trying to meet the approval of both their girlfriend and their friends? If I'd spent time with Michael and Dan when they were sixteen-year-olds, hanging out with the other guys from their school, they probably would have been doing just that. Trying to be cool and trying to give the girl what she wants. Putting on an act for one or the other, or maybe both.

I shouldn't be critical of Eddie for this. I mean, everyone pretends a little bit. My own behaviour around the school crowd probably wouldn't hold up under close scrutiny. But I don't pretend around him. Or at least I didn't until – well, until recently.

Or maybe I just didn't realise that I was pretending until recently.

I look at my own menu and tell myself that it's all ok and it's all going to be fine and I'm just in a weird kind of mood and then I look over at Eddie again and it's not all ok.

I don't want to be here.

"I kissed Michael." The words are out of my mouth before I have a chance to think about it.

It's right at that moment the waiter comes over to take our order. For a second I think Eddie's going to snap in some way – yell at the waiter, yell at me, run out of here. But he just says, very calmly, that he'll have a tea, and I'm left flustered, trying to remember whether I wanted chocolate ice-cream or a chocolate brownie or something in between. I end up ordering an apple Danish because it's the first thing that catches my eye when I look desperately at the menu, and forget to tell the waiter I want coffee.

"When?" Eddie asks the second the waiter has put his pen down.

"At my party. After you left." There is something so unreal about giving these details to Eddie. Time seems to be moving just a little more slowly than usual.

He's looking at me expectantly. What am I supposed to say? What can I say? And then I remember.

"I know it was – really wrong of me. It just happened."

Is that what he wants? I can't tell.

He nods slowly. "I'm glad you told me," he says, and then puts his hand over his mouth and stares determinedly at the menu.

"Are you ok?" I ask after a few minutes, not sure how to interpret this behaviour.

"You kissed someone else, Kim, of course I'm not ok," he mutters.

The waiter approaches again with our tray, and it occurs to me that I'm going to have to sit here with Eddie until I finish eating. I really need to work on my timing.

And I don't even like my apple Danish. It's too soggy and too sweet. Pastries are unrelentingly sweet; chocolate concoctions have that edge to the sweetness. I prod what's left of it with my fork and decide to leave it.

"Are you going to have that?" I ask Eddie, who still hasn't poured his tea.

"Oh. Right," he says, and starts pouring, and then puts in sugar even though to the best of my knowledge he never takes sugar in his tea. It takes him several gulps to realise that there's something wrong, and he looks at the mug in bewilderment.

Guilt pokes me sharply in my chest. I've broken him. Or at least am responsible for that undrinkable cup of tea.

"I'm sorry," I say, and I really mean it. I'm sorry he's sitting there looking so miserable. I'm sorry I'm the one that caused all of this. I am sorry.

Do I even have the right to be the one here while he's upset? I mean, what good is that going to do? He should go talk to his friends or something, assuming boys are there for each other in the same way girls are after a break-up.

"I should go," I say, and am fishing for my wallet so that I can pay for my food when he says something that surprises me.

"No, don't, we should talk about this now," he says.

"There's something to talk about?" I say, another thing that escapes my mouth without being filtered through my brain.

Eddie's talking about how we can get through this, how he'll get over it eventually even though it's going to be hard, how he loves me, how we're strong enough to make it through this.

He has so much confidence in us, and I had us broken up already.

I could go along with this. I could stay with him. Suddenly the option of being completely honest with him *and* staying with him is there. He can still be my boyfriend. What happened with Michael doesn't have to destroy that.

Everything can go back to the way it was and everything *can* be ok.

I look at Eddie as he talks and I take a breath before saying what a million other people have said before. "I don't think it's going to work out between us."

He stops talking, and I examine the corner of the menu very thoroughly, picking at where the laminate is coming off.

"Are you saying that because of Michael?" he finally asks.

"It's not about him," I say.

"Because – if you're serious about this, Kim, then this is final. I'm not going to be here if you change your mind."

"I'm serious," I say, and now I look at him. He seems so solemn.

"Ok," he says, as though he doesn't believe me, and then gets up and walks out.

That tone, that sure-of-himself tone as though he's absolutely positive I'm going to call him and change my mind and throw myself at his feet, is enough to get me home without crying. I'm angry, not anything else, angry at his patronising tone and the notion that I'm making a foolish mistake here. How dare he, how *dare* he!

And then I get home and everything is so normal. Dan is sitting at the kitchen table with his Irish book open talking to Jim about what the exam is like and what kind of stuff comes up, and Mum's reading the newspaper and drinking coffee despite it really being too late for it, and when I come in she pours me some and I sit down and listen to Dan go on about paper one and paper two and the listening bit and what the hardest part is.

I can't be angry here. All I am is calm, and reasonable, thinking about things like how it's probably just as well Eddie and I never ventured into the land of no-clothes, and that I never borrow anything from him and therefore have nothing to give back to him. I am glad that he gave me the kind of birthday present that doesn't last – the chocolates were shared at the party, the roses are ready to be thrown out – so that I don't feel obliged to return anything.

I'm thinking about how I probably won't go to the New Year's party this year, because Eddie will be there, but that's no great tragedy. Even though I could go, and flirt with and kiss whoever I wanted to, and it would be ok, because I don't have a boyfriend any more. I'm free for the first time this year, able to do what I want without taking someone else into account.

"What did you and Eddie go and see?" Mum asks.

"*Getting Over You*," I say. "It's rubbish."

"The reviews weren't great," Jim nods, taking a moment away from the in-depth analysis of the examining of the Irish language at Leaving Certificate level.

"Mmm." I pause, and consider. Should I tell them, that's it? It's really over. It's really, seriously, no-going-back over. I'm not going to tell them only to have to sheepishly correct them a few days down the line.

But then again, Eddie said it was over for good. Final. He said it was final. That is not a word that you use when things might change in a few days' time.

It's still not real enough to say yet.

I go up to bed instead. My phone beeps just as I'm hunting for the perfect CD to fall asleep to, and I jump.

It's Eddie. I stare at his name at the top of the message for ages, wondering what he has to say, wondering if he's going to be angry and demand an actual explanation for why we are no longer together, wondering if he just wants everything to be ok and go back to normal between us.

He wants to know if I'm sure.

I don't even let myself think about it. I send the message and then turn my phone off.

Yes, I'm sure.

It's not entirely true, but it's close enough to be what I need to tell him, and myself, before I can fall asleep.

20

Cry-baby

On Thursday I'm a robot, answering yes and no at the right moments without really thinking about anything. After lunch I have an accounting module with Dawn – it's our last one ever, what with the term ending soon, so we're supposed to be filling out sheets with what we learned over the last few months and whether we want to take this subject for Leaving Cert and all that stuff.

It doesn't surprise me that Dawn is more interested in talking than writing down how fascinating the art of book-keeping is, but what does surprise me is that she asks me, "Kim – is everything ok with you and Eddie?"

"Yeah," I lie, "everything's fine."

Except once I've said that, I can feel just how not-fine it is. And I try to smile but I can't.

"Really?" she says knowingly.

"Um. Actually it's – we're – it's over. We broke up."

She assumes the sympathetic look that I have seen her wear so many times before. Strangely, now that it's directed at me, it feels genuine. "Oh my God, what happened?"

And I tell her. "It just didn't feel right any more. You know?"

She nods. "Yeah. There's nothing you can do about that. You're better off breaking up with him."

"Mmmm," I say, and wonder how it is that Dawn can give me that kind of advice when she never takes it herself.

How often do I actually listen to my own advice, though? Maybe if I did all my thinking out loud I'd be just like her. So she falls for other guys when in a relationship – I *kissed* one.

"And then there's this other guy," I say, because even though I don't want to be like Dawn it's hard to see the point in pretending we've nothing in common, "who I really like."

"Is that why you and Eddie are over?"

I consider this. "No. We'd have been over anyway, eventually. But the guy – he's not talking to me at the moment."

Last Saturday night I was, for a very brief moment, a girl with two guys interested in her – or at least, one interested and one willing to be kissed. One can be enough to inspire envy, and two – well, if this was happening to someone else, I'd find it very hard to feel sorry for them. In my head, I know all that, but it's hard to go from that to having no guys in such a short space of time.

Because in the abstract it's 'no guys' and that's not the end of the world by a long stretch, but then for practical purposes it means that I don't have an Eddie to call at any hour of the night and talk to, an Eddie to put his arm around me and kiss me and just be there, and I don't have a Michael to sit down and have coffee with and laugh with.

The image of him pushing a mug of hot coffee across the table to me, followed by a tissue, comes to my mind. After Tom. Just the two of us in my kitchen. It was the end of the summer. I was fourteen.

He was a few months older than Eddie is now. I try to imagine what Eddie would do in that situation. Hug the sobbing girl, probably. Stroke her hair. All reasonable, nice, gentlemanly things to do.

But I didn't want to be touched, right then. Because a girl who's right out of a relationship that ended because of touching-related issues – how much how fast how soon can we hop into bed now please –

doesn't want to be reminded of how it feels to be touched, especially by someone who's not the guy she was, honestly, crazy about.

He knew that. I forget whether I might have given him any indication, maybe flinched at some moment when he brushed against me, but he knew, or he picked up on it, and he *got* me.

"Sweetie, are you ok?"

I've been staring into space. "Oh. Yeah. Well, no."

When the bell goes, and we're supposed to be on our way to our history class to hear about how we can get started on our family trees, I get my schoolbag and sneak out of the school via the fire door that doesn't work any more. It leads out into a walled-off green area, so there hasn't been too much pressure to get it sorted out – the assumption is, I think, that girls in pleated skirts are not the greatest or most willing climbers. Girls trying to slip out of school early are more likely to risk timing their escape to coincide with the receptionist's tea breaks.

But I just want to get out of here, and there's nothing like a childhood of chasing around boys to hone your wall-climbing skills.

I land on the other side of the wall in one piece, more or less, and begin the walk home. It's only a few minutes away, but the tears are already falling by the time I'm hunting in my pockets for my keys.

Bursting into tears repeatedly is exhausting. Every time I've mopped up my eyes and prepared to get on with my life and stop being so miserable, something else hits me. The smell of coffee makes me cry. That photo in the kitchen. Ads on TV with girls flirting with boys and boys pursuing girls and happy wrinkled old married-for-fifty-years couples.

By the time Dan gets home from school, I feel as though I'm too wrecked to cry any more, but then the way my heart pauses when the key turns in the door and I stick my head downstairs to see if Michael's with him, and the way it sinks when it's just Dan on his own – well, that's enough to start me off again.

I stay in my room and listen to the Hero Librarians' first album. I sob my way through tracks two (the first song I heard after getting together with Tom), four (the song Michael played for me to get me hooked on this group), six (one of the songs I had on repeat in the early days of Eddie), seven (residual crying from the previous song) and nine (for its insightful lyrics concerning love and loss).

By track eleven, the fine art of wallowing is rapidly losing its appeal.

I move into productive mode instead. I tidy my room thoroughly for the second time in the space of a week. I put my CDs into order again, this time sorting by genres that make sense to me – embarrassingly cheesy pop music, cheesy pop music from so long ago that it's sort of cool now, good soundtracks from bad movies, bad soundtracks from good movies, by-the-numbers rock music, weird-but-interesting rock music, weird-just-plain-weird rock music, girls with guitars singing about boys, girls with guitars singing about the wrongs of the world, dead-and-forever-pretty rock gods, music to sing around a campfire, soundtracks from musicals, greatest hits collections from bands who can fit all their good songs on one or two CDs.

Once I've transferred the stacks of CDs into various corners of the rack, I start on Christmas present lists. When I look at my calendar I'm shocked that Christmas is next week, that it's so soon, as though there isn't the same distance between my birthday and Christmas every single year.

I make a list of family and friends. Mum, Dad, Jim, Annelise. Annelise always says that I shouldn't get her anything but I like buying her things. Mum always has to tell me what to get for Jim, usually something boring like a history book or a classical CD, but Annelise is easy to buy for – things that are cute without being tacky, like scented candles with patterns running up the side. Dan. Elaine, Bonnie, Deirdre. I add Michael to the list at the end, in small neat letters.

I started my Christmas shopping in November.

When I take out the big bag from the back of my wardrobe, and begin matching up presents to names, I have something for everyone on the list already. Once I throw in a few chocolate Santas to compensate for some of the gifts being less extravagant than others, I'll be finished.

I check the bag to see if there's anything left in it. There isn't.

Of course, back in November, I'd just bought a birthday present for him a few weeks previously. But still – in all that time wandering around shops, picking up little bits and pieces that I thought would be perfect for Elaine, or for Michael, or even my dad's 'lady friend', I didn't buy anything for my boyfriend.

I think about how much effort I put into his birthday present, and then I wonder if he actually might have put as much effort into mine.

There's a big difference between putting in effort to find the perfect gift, and putting in effort to determine what the perfect gift might be.

Back in *November*, I still wasn't sure enough about Eddie to buy him something that he'd like.

Dawn's right. We're better off broken up.

I accompany Jim on his usual big Thursday night supermarket expedition and pick out chocolate Santas. I pause in front of the display of Selection Boxes and get one for Dan, because in recent years well-meaning relatives have foolishly believed both of us too old for such things.

When I catch up with Jim he's looking at wines.

"What are those for?" I ask as he adds two bottles of red wine to his trolley.

"Saturday," he says, holding up another bottle and reading the label on the back. I am familiar with that brand. It's dreadful. It's probably best not to share that information with Jim, though. Besides, maybe real wine-drinkers would like it and I'm just not cultured enough to appreciate it.

"What's on Saturday?" All I know about Saturday is that I'm baby-sitting that afternoon. What's Jim up to?

"The Christmas party," Jim says in a tone you might use to tell someone what their own name is. It's understandable, seeing as the Christmas party – in the same vein as Christmas itself – happens at this time every year. It's not even a party so much as a low-key get-together – a handful of people from Mum and Jim's work, a few relatives, a few neighbours, Michael. Mum and Dad hardly ever had people over around Christmas when they were together; I think it's Jim's way of making his mark on our calendar. And his chance to pretend to be a comedian for a night.

I'm not sure if I'll be particularly in the mood to talk to people about school and other socially-acceptable things on Saturday night. Then again, if Michael's there –

Right. Because he's going to come over to the house for a social event when he's not speaking to me.

But he might. Maybe. He always comes.

The possibility is enough to keep smiling all the way through wrapping everyone's presents. The tags attached have messages scrawled on them that are more cheerful than you'd expect from someone who's just broken up with her boyfriend.

21

Baby-sitter

By the second class on Friday morning everyone knows that Eddie and I have broken up. Telling Dawn something really is like announcing it over the intercom. At break I'm quiet for a split second and everyone jumps on the are-you-ok bandwagon.

"I'm fine," I say repeatedly, which is partially true. I'm not heartbroken over Eddie, but I am sad that it's over – on the other hand, Michael is the one occupying my mind during these brief silences.

Bonnie corners me at lunch and we go through all the gory details, all the things Dawn and the rest of them don't know because it involves explaining that actually I kissed that boy I'm interested in.

I take her up on her offer of keeping me company

on Friday night, and we work our way through her extensive sitcoms-on-DVD collection until three in the morning.

"We haven't done this in ages," she says sleepily, curled up in a sleeping bag on the couch.

I'm on the floor trying to remember the last time we actually had a DVD night. A real one, not just lying to the parents and telling them that was what we were doing. "Yeah," is the only response I can think of.

"Kim?"

"Yeah?"

"Are you and Dawn suddenly best friends?"

"What?"

"I mean – she didn't even come to your party, you know? So how come she knew about you and Eddie before everyone else?"

"She just – asked if something was going on. It wasn't like I decided to tell her first or anything." I sit up. "She only has a vague outline, anyway. She doesn't know the whole story."

"Ok." She pauses. "I just miss being your talk-to person."

"You're still my talk-to person."

"Really?"

I smile. "Really. Go to sleep."

I'm tired, but I stay awake for a while, glad that she's here, glad that I have friends.

In the morning, really closer to afternoon, she leaves to go help Vodka Drinker Number One with his Christmas shopping, and Mum gives me a lift over to Allie's.

"Kim!" Aisling, at four, is still enthusiastic enough about baby-sitters to run to the door for a hug, while Jane is too cool for such things and sits on the stairs reading.

Allie's going to be home around half six. It is now twenty to two. I'm glad I've already had coffee.

Jane shows me the drawings she's done and tells me about how much homework they get in third class. Aisling tugs on my sleeve and demands that we read a story.

"Go *away*," Jane says, glaring. "I'm showing Kim my pictures."

"They're stupid pictures," Aisling says, making a face.

I intervene. "Aisling, that's not nice. Say sorry."

Aisling sulks when I don't take her side. She storms off into the next room.

"How are you at drawing people?" I ask Jane.

She shrugs. "Ok."

"How about you do a portrait of me and Aisling?"

"I don't want to draw *Aisling*."

"Come on, you're the big girl, you know she's just being a baby. She can't help it, she's four."

"I wasn't like that when I was four," she says firmly.

"Yeah, but you're the oldest. The oldest ones are always more mature." I wonder if this holds true for me and Dan. I feel more mature than I remember him being at sixteen.

"What's mature?"

"Grown-up."

Jane considers this. "But she's so *annoying*."

"I bet she'd be fun to draw, though."

I tell Aisling I'll read to her, but first she has to apologise to her sister. We eventually get settled in the playroom, with Aisling leaning into me as I read her a story, funny voices included, and Jane set up next to us like a professional painter, with a miniature easel and everything.

After that we play board games and then they demonstrate how to use several new toys that have been purchased since the last time I was here. I envy the younger generation for their cooler toys. We never had anything this fancy when I was little. I feel like I've had a horribly deprived childhood. Aisling has this really cool construction set made out of bright primary-coloured magnetic pieces, and they have this stuff that's like Play-Doh except it's made out of foam. And the Crayola range has expanded even more – I used to think magic markers were cool, where you'd draw over something with your special white pen and it'd change colour, but Jane has a set that lets you draw on black paper. Sometimes when kids are showing you things, you have to feign interest, but with these I'm truly captivated.

I wonder if I'd get too many odd looks if I went into a toyshop to purchase some of these things for myself. Kids' toys are *brilliant*. We're still happily playing by the time Allie arrives home.

I'd have stayed later, I realise, if she'd asked. Despite the lack of sleep, despite the boy-related crap going on, I would have.

Why did I think I wanted to be a teacher? Was it just because Dad is always saying what a handy degree it is, because he's been nudging me towards it? There are so many other ways to work with kids, there's a world outside the classroom. There are possibilities out there that I can't even imagine right now because I'm still stuck in school. I might still teach, but it's not my only option. I can work with kids without being in a school all day dealing with Pearl-like children.

Why is it that, even when you know on some level what you're going to end up doing, you get distracted along the way and get caught up in things you don't want? Why does it feel like you want them even though it's not going to last?

I take my mp3 player out of my bag and select the playlist that has 'My Dream Boy' on it. I walk home humming the tune.

22

Fashion Victim

Everything I have is wrong. I do not own a single item of wearable clothing. How is it that I am sixteen years old and my mother has a better wardrobe than I do?

People start coming over at around eight for this Christmas party thing. It's seven-thirty and everything I have makes me look dumpy or awkward or so-obviously-young-trying-to-look-older. I can't wear the red dress. I hate the red dress. Actually, I love the red dress, but it doesn't look good on me. I think it clashes with my hair. Or maybe my skin tones. There's clashing going on, at any rate.

I can't find a single colour that suits me. I have garments in various shades of fuchsia and turquoise and peach and crimson and lemon and teal and burgundy and nothing works. I have more colours in my wardrobe than Jane has in her gigantic colouring pencil set (it comes in a *suitcase*, for God's sake) and none of them are calling out to me and hinting that maybe they might make me look reasonably attractive tonight.

I hate my skin. Are paper bags still in? What's the verdict on the paper bag look for this season?

I'm being ridiculous. I know I'm being ridiculous. The knowledge is not stopping me from going slightly insane.

Black. Black is always good. Except I can't wear the black outfit from my birthday because then it'll seem as though I only have one decent outfit and even though boys never really notice what girls are wearing, I am pretty sure Michael will remember that I was wearing this only a week ago.

I don't even know if he's definitely coming. I could be getting myself all worked up for nothing.

I don't know why I'm even bothering, anyway. First there's the issue of him not speaking to me, and then there's the way he's seen me in all kinds of unattractive clothing before. Old jumpers that should have been thrown out years ago, outfits my mother picked out for me when I was a kid, my first bikini. How much of a difference can one single outfit make?

But if I were to look good tonight, be the kind of

attractive girl that sixteen-year-olds are supposed to be – then it would make a difference.

So I keep pawing through my clothes to see if I can find something that will make me happy. Maybe a fairy godmother will step out of the wardrobe bearing something that I have forgotten about, some fantastic dress that'll make me look all slender and willowy or some classy top that will transform me into elegance personified.

I know what I really need is a fairy godmother to transform me into someone Michael will talk to rather than be angry with. I know that. But the right outfit seems like a reasonable step in that direction.

Except that I have nothing to wear. Which is such a traditional girly thing to say that I'm rolling my eyes at myself even as I think it. Because of course I have things to wear. It's just that none of them are *right*.

The doorbell rings twice while I'm sitting on my bed staring into space.

I try on the red dress for the fifth time and pull my hair away from my face as I look in the mirror. It looks ok. I suppose. I have to wear something. Objectivity and perspective have run away screaming at this stage but I know that this dress is appropriate for the occasion, at least.

I then move on to worrying about the appropriateness of my shoes for ten minutes. Mum sticks her head around the door to check if I'm going to be coming downstairs soon.

"I'll be down soon," I say, and slip my feet into these shoes in what is meant to be a decisive gesture but just ends up hurting my toes.

I tie back my hair and glare at my reflection. A layer of foundation later and I look presentable but not like me. I hate wearing make-up – it feels weird and it's such an ordeal putting it on and then having to take it off again later.

I wash my face, dab a tiny bit of concealer over a particularly atrocious disaster zone on my forehead, and remind myself that there is no point in pretending to be someone or something I'm not just to get someone else interested in me. I remind myself that I used to believe in that and that drifting away from such principles is the reason I found myself in a relationship where I didn't even know what to buy the guy for Christmas.

I remind myself that Michael knows what I look like and that it doesn't make a difference if I'm not perfect. I remind myself that this is a gorgeous dress and that it alone is worthy of awe, regardless of the body it's hanging from.

Sure enough, as I walk down the stairs, someone actually says, "Oh wow, that's such a gorgeous dress!"

I smile and say thanks before it hits me that I know

that girl. I look at her. She's pretty – dark curly hair, slim, maybe a year or two older than I am or else just possessing an air of sophistication that I lack.

The name's on my tongue before I realise I need to stop running through groups in my head and trying to figure out whether she's in school with me or whether she was in the Gaeltacht or what.

"Hey, Caitriona," I say, contemplating running back up to my room and hiding out there for the rest of the night. Why else would she be here if not because of Michael?

And sure enough, Michael is leaving the kitchen and approaching us as we speak.

"Hi," he says to both of us. At least he's speaking to me. That's something.

"Mike. Hey. How're you doing?" Caitriona asks, sounding at ease but not overly intimate. Maybe they're not back together.

He shrugs.

"Seeing anyone?" she says.

"Yeah," he says.

What?

"She's here tonight," he continues, and I think he means me. I really do. My face is ready to light up when a girl emerges from the kitchen, sees him, and slips right into place at his side. His arm curves around her.

I know that girl, too.

My stupid mouth is still escaping from that hopeful joyful almost-smile as Michael introduces Caitriona to Elaine.

23

Spectator

I flee to my room as soon as I can think of an excuse – I need to get my phone – and as soon as I feel able to verbalise that excuse without bursting into tears.

Michael. Elaine. Arms. Touching. Couple.

How could I have been such an idiot, thinking that they weren't together just because they weren't all over each other as they came downstairs at my birthday party? They gave me a joint present, for God's sake. I'm an *idiot.*

I can't believe he brought my friend to my family's Christmas party a week after I kissed him. If I was looking for a sign that he wasn't interested – well, that's about as pointed as it gets, I suppose.

And about as harsh as you can get when you want

to remind someone that their feelings don't actually matter. I mean, I knew Michael was annoyed with me, but Elaine? Elaine is supposed to be my friend. She's told me twice, now, that Michael likes me, when clearly it's her he's interested in, and what kind of a friend does something like that?

Maybe she's just been using me to get to know Michael better.

I am just so *stupid.*

I feel like a kid who all the grown-ups humour, like everyone's winking at each other over my head. At least when you're a kid and you have bad friends, your parents step in and get involved, talk to you or talk to the friend or talk to their parents or get your teacher to separate the two of you during school. You're not expected to have enough sense to know who makes a good friend and who makes a bad friend.

And now I'm sixteen and I apparently still can't tell the difference. I was thinking *Dawn* wasn't the greatest person in the world, and it turns out even she's a better friend than Elaine.

I sit in the bathroom with damp tissue paper clumped over my eyes for five minutes in the hope that it'll take the edge off the teary redness. When I look in the mirror I'm not sure I can see that much of a difference, but I'm closer to being able to go downstairs and behave in an appropriately festive manner.

Family parties like this are usually nothing to worry about. I know what my function is. When I go downstairs, I hang around with the grown-ups first of all, and know exactly where I fit in. I'm Kate's daughter, Jim's stepdaughter, Sarah's baby cousin, Richard's niece.

I answer questions about how school is going, the importance of Transition Year as a time-out in this exam-obsessed educational system, contemporary music, and where I bought my dress. In between explaining to Richard exactly what Transition Year is and trying to make it sound as though it is a valid and worthwhile way of spending one's time in school, I glance over at the couch. The couch is where this stops being a laid-back event and starts being something stressful. The couch is where Michael is sitting, with Elaine perched on his knee exactly the same way I was seven days ago, talking to Dan and Caitriona and another girl.

Elaine catches my eye and waves me over, as though nothing is wrong and we're all friends here. I'm perfectly happy to stay here talking to people who haven't run off with Michael, but Richard notices and shoos me over to where the "young people" are.

I sit down on the armrest, next to Dan, and he introduces me to the girl beside him. "Kim, this is Saoirse. Saoirse, this is my sister, Kim."

Saoirse is the first girl Dan has ever invited over to something like this. Normally the plan involves keeping the girlfriends far far away from the relatives and Mum and Jim's work crowd, not to mention Mum and Jim themselves.

They're talking about a film I haven't seen yet, the one I was hoping to go to with Eddie. I shake my head and say I haven't seen it and sit quietly as they discuss it.

Michael won't look at me. He has his arms looped around Elaine's waist, and she has her hands resting on where his hands meet. He nods in agreement with Caitriona's comment that the scene with the wishing well could have been better (I'm completely lost) and leans in closer to Elaine to kiss her on the cheek.

I breathe in and out.

Even when Michael and Caitriona were together, he was never overly affectionate with her in public. Then again, maybe I didn't notice, back then. Maybe I wasn't watching them this carefully.

Elaine looks at me and smiles. I pretend I don't notice. Does she really expect me to be thrilled for her?

I watch the two of them, and then Dan and Saoirse. Saoirse takes Dan's hand and brushes her thumb over his knuckles. When he acknowledges the gesture, slipping his fingers in between hers, she glows.

That is what I want with Michael.

This couch is far too coupley for my liking. I watch Caitriona, sitting in between Elaine-and-Michael and Dan-and-Saoirse. She shifts a little, as though she's awkward, but maybe I'm projecting my own discomfort onto her.

What is she doing here, anyway, if she's not with Michael?

"I'm going to get another drink," Elaine says. "Anyone want anything?" Michael releases his hold on her, and I follow her to the kitchen. To help her carry things.

"So you and Julian," I say as I get cans of Coke out of the fridge. "What happened there?"

"We're going to give it a try," she says. She frowns. "I told you that before, didn't I?"

I stare at her.

"Are you ok?" she asks.

"No!" I splutter. "You – and Michael – *and* Julian? What – I don't – what are you doing?"

Elaine laughs. "Kim!" she says.

"I don't want to hear it," I say, ready to retreat to my room. I can't believe she's laughing at me.

She grabs my arm. "Hey. Listen. You know earlier, when you said you were getting your phone – you didn't, did you?"

"What are you talking about?"

"I sent you a message. Look – you know what's

going on, right?"

"Yeah, you and Michael decided you're perfect for each other. How long has that been going on for, huh?"

I only realise I've been shouting when Elaine pointedly closes the door into the next room. "We're not together, hon," she says. "He's just trying to make his ex jealous."

This is even more confusing than the conversation about the film. "Caitriona? Why did she even come?"

"Ok. So Dan was bringing his girlfriend, right? And she wanted to bring her friend, which he said was fine, but then he's over at her house this afternoon and the friend comes over to get ready and it's Caitriona. He texts Michael to tell him, Michael calls me and asks if I'll pretend to be his girlfriend for the night. He's going to burn a whole bunch of CDs for me – it's not a bad deal."

It takes a moment for it to sink in. "Oh. So you and Michael aren't –"

"Do I have to remind you again that he's crazy about you?"

I stare at the floor. "If he's so crazy about me then why didn't he get *me* to pretend to be his girlfriend?"

"Because you have a boyfriend! Where is he, anyway?"

"He's not my boyfriend any more," I say.

Elaine's mouth actually falls open in shock. "Ok. Sit

down. Tell me what happened."

We sit at the kitchen table, setting down the cans next to a plate of mince pies.

I decide it is probably best to omit the part where Michael and I were trying to eavesdrop on her and Julian, and skip to the kiss, then the anger, then the telling of Eddie and the realisation that even if the kiss didn't make him want to break up with me, I needed to end things with him.

"You do like him. Michael, I mean. You do, don't you?" Elaine looks intently at me.

I nod. "Yeah."

"You should tell him," she says, quoting my own advice back at me.

I sigh. Right now I don't feel capable of telling anyone anything important. And anyway, I kissed him. If that isn't telling him, I don't know what is, and look how well that turned out.

Elaine brings out the drinks for the couch-dwellers and I go up to my room to actually get my phone. Sure enough, there's a message advising me to play along with her being Michael's girlfriend for the night. At least Elaine isn't evil and horrible. At least I have my friends. I have Elaine, and I have Bonnie – I don't need a boy, right? It's not a crisis for me to be single.

But Michael *is* my friend. Or he was one, back in the days when he wasn't pretending I don't exist.

It's a Christmas party. Maybe I should make a tear-jerking toast to friendship and love and hope that he gets the message. But I hate public speaking and those kinds of speeches are sort of soppy, anyway.

I rejoin the couch crowd and decide I'm just going to try to patch things up with Michael and then we can be friends again and we can forget all of this crap. I don't like being neurotic and crazy and worrying about clothes and getting jealous of his fake girlfriend (even now, when I know they're only pretending, I'm still envious of Elaine's position on his lap) and all the rest. I don't want to be that girl. I want to be the old Kim, all calm and sensible and reasonable.

Of course, the old Kim was far too fond of putting up with things that maybe she shouldn't have. So possibly the new-old Kim will be more aware of any developing alienation between herself and her new boyfriend. Better yet, the new-old Kim will wait a very long time before she gets into another relationship.

It seems like an excellent plan. No more stress, no more tears.

I watch the way Michael's hand rests on Elaine's arm, just below her elbow, and doubt the feasibility of this plan.

They've moved on to discussing what they're putting down on their CAO forms, Dan talking about whether or not he should stick down medicine as his first choice or if it'd be foolish because he's convinced he won't get the points for it.

"It's Saturday night. I can't believe we're talking about this," Michael says, but in a good-natured sort of way.

"Just put it down," Saoirse says, for what I suspect is not the first time. "You know you want it."

Because that's how the system works. Dan has explained it to us several hundred times over dinner. If you know what you want, the one course you know is right for you, you put it at number one on the list. Maybe you won't get the points for it, but it's better to have it as an option than to eliminate it straight away.

It occurs to me that Dan's problem is not that he can't decide what he wants to do. He's been talking about medicine for years, in the same way that I've known for ages that I want to work with kids. It's just that it's easier to talk and worry and debate than it is to admit what you want and try to – and maybe fail to – get it.

"Michael," I say, "can I talk to you for a minute?"

24

Action Figure

Michael looks at me properly for the first time all night. "Now?"

"Yeah."

Elaine is smiling. Caitriona looks curious.

"Can't it wait?" he says in a voice verging on angry.

I am polite but pointed. "Don't worry, your girlfriend will be fine without you for a few minutes."

He takes the hint and gets up before I reveal that it's all a lie. I lead the way out into the hall.

I'm leaning against the door to the study and it's almost as though we've been catapulted back into last week, except for the impatience on his face.

"What is it?" he asks.

I look at him and I don't know where to begin, what

the right words are. The language of attraction is all about touching and feeling, about kisses and hugs, and I'm afraid that if I try to touch him he'll push me away.

"So, you and Elaine, huh?" I say casually.

"That's what you want to talk about?"

"So you want to get back with Caitriona?"

He is silent for a moment. "Do you really think that's any of your business?"

"You're using my friend to make her jealous, so, yeah, I think it's my business." I hate that we're doing this, that we're almost-fighting out here.

"I'm not sure she's the one who's jealous," he says.

"Oh, well done, Michael, I'm jealous!" I snap. "Of course I am – you're all over her like –"

"Like what?"

"Like nothing happened between us!"

He glares. "Oh, right, you mean when you kissed me? When you, who's practically *married* to Eddie, got bored or fed up or whatever and decided, hey, Mikey hasn't got any in ages, he's all pathetic and lonely, he won't mind if I use him!"

"No, I kissed you when *I*, who *broke up* with Eddie by the way, realised that actually I'm crazy about you, and it has nothing to do with using you, you *idiot*!"

We stare at each other.

"Are we finished fighting?" I ask quietly.

"I think so," he says. "You broke up with Eddie?"

"Yeah. You really thought I was *using* you?"

He shrugs. "It seemed like a possibility."

I look at him, and it hits me how messy kisses can make friendships. For Michael and me to be having a conversation like this, for us not to be understanding one another – it feels strange and unnatural.

"Mikey? I wouldn't ever do that. Ever."

He nods.

"Um. Do you – do you want to get back with Caitriona?"

He leans against the wall and answers the question in the same voice he would have used if I'd asked before all of this happened. "It's just that she always asks me if I'm with anyone. Every time I see her."

"So why did you call Elaine?"

He shrugs. "I wouldn't have thought of it, but you said, at your party, you thought there was something going on between me and her – "

"So you knew that it'd be convincing," I fill in.

He's silent for a minute. "Yeah. Actually, I thought it might convince you, as well. It was stupid, I just thought that – I don't know."

"It worked. I was convinced."

"So," he says.

"So," I say.

"We should head back inside."

"Right," I say, but before we do that I lean in and hug him, tightly. We're there when Richard walks out, raises an eyebrow, and makes us uncomfortable, as though we've been caught doing something far more inappropriate than hugging. He goes into the bathroom and Michael and I look at each other.

"Inside," I say.

"Yeah," he says.

Back inside, sitting on the couch, he grins at me and I grin back and we're friends again and everything's back to normal. Everything's ok. It's not strange and unnatural, or awkward and tense.

By the end of the night, I've just about talked myself into the idea that neither of us is ready to jump into anything new, if he's still trying to prove something to his ex-girlfriend and if I'm only just out of a relationship.

On the other hand, if we both know what the other is really like – that I would kiss someone I wasn't going out with, that he would get a fake girlfriend to inspire envy in not one but two other girls – and still like each other, it'd be foolish to not do something, wouldn't it?

At the end of the night, after all the 'young people' and a considerable portion of the adults have gone home, when Dan is walking Saoirse home, it's just me and Michael on the couch, and I am dithering between doing what is sensible and doing what I want to do.

He makes it easy, this time. "So what's Santa bringing you?" he asks.

"I asked him for a nice boy. I don't know if there are any left in the world, though."

"The elves might make one for you," he says, moving in closer.

"Maybe," I say, "I hear they're very –"

And then he's kissing me, and I could care less about elves, Santa, or standard post-break-up procedure. He's kissing me, and the only thing I have room for in my head is sheer exhilaration.

When Dan arrives home we're all snuggled up together on the couch. He takes one look at us, rolls his eyes, and says, "Move over, I want to watch TV."

Epilogue

The thing about birthdays, about Christmas, about any day that comes around once a year, is that it's the time when you reflect on your life. You think about the people in your life, your relationships, your priorities. You think about the kind of person you want to be, and the kind of person you are, and how to make those two ideas match up a little bit more.

I am that girl who kisses boys when she's going out with someone else, and I know enough now to understand that it's never as simple as you'd think from looking on from outside. I am that girl who gets involved with someone else days after ending one relationship even though she's aware that most people wouldn't consider it the wisest move to make. I am that girl who wants to take action instead of worry, to go after what she wants instead of thinking too much about things.

I am sixteen years old and, for the most part, I am happy.

And being that girl is something I can definitely live with.

THE END

Published 2007
by Poolbeg Press Ltd
123 Grange Hill, Baldoyle
Dublin 13, Ireland
E-mail: poolbeg@poolbeg.com

1 3 5 7 9 10 8 6 4 2

A catalogue record for this book is available from the British Library.

ISBN 978-1-84223-288-0

Typeset by Type Design in Palatino 11.5/15.5
Printed by
Litografia Rosés, Spain

www.poolbeg.com

That girl

Claire Hennessy

POOLBEG